The Cat
Canary

A Melodrama in Three Acts

by John Willard

A SAMUEL FRENCH ACTING EDITION

SAMUEL FRENCH

FOUNDED 1830

New York Hollywood London Toronto

SAMUELFRENCH.COM

THE PEOPLE IN THE PLAY

(In the order in which they speak.)

MAMMY PLEASANT, *old negress.*
ROGER CROSBY, *the lawyer.*
HARRY BLYTHE.
CICILY YOUNG.
SUSAN SILLSBY.
CHARLIE WILDER.
PAUL JONES.
ANNABELLE WEST.
HENDRICKS, *guard at asylum.*
PATTERSON.

SYNOPSIS

The action takes place at Glencliff Manor on the Hudson—is practically continuous.

ACT I: *Library. Eleven-thirty. Night.*
ACT II: *The next room. A few minutes later.*
ACT III: *Library. A few minutes later.*

3

The following is a copy of the program of the first performance of "THE CAT AND THE CANARY," as produced at the National Theatre, New York, February 7, 1922.

KILBOURN GORDON, INC.

Presents

"THE CAT AND THE CANARY"

A Melodrama in Three Acts

By JOHN WILLARD

CAST OF CHARACTERS

ROGER CROSBY....................*Percy Moore*
"MAMMY" PLEASANT..........*Blanche Friderici*
HARRY BLYTHE....................*John Willard*
SUSAN SILLSBY... ....*Beth Franklin*
CICELY YOUNG.................*Jane Warrington*
CHARLES WILDER.................*Ryder Keane*
PAUL JONES.......................*Henry Hull*
ANNABELLE WEST.............*Florence Eldredge*
HENDRICKS......................*Edmund Elton*
PATTERSON.................*Harry D. Southard*

The Cat and the Canary

ACT I

SCENE: *Library at Glencliff Manor.*
TIME: *About eleven-thirty in the evening.*
A large, old-fashioned room, full of dark corners and shadows.
Door L. *High-backed couch* R., *bookcases line the walls at back.*
AT RISE: MAMMY *enters—followed by* CROSBY. *Lights stage* R. *are on.*

CROSBY. (*An old family lawyer. He looks at his watch*) A little more light, Mammy, please. (MAMMY *lights lamp table* L. CROSBY *looking around.*) That's better. Well, the old place looks just the same.

MAMMY. (*Closes door*) Yes, sir—nothing's been changed here in twenty years.

CROSBY. You've been faithful to your trust, Mammy.

MAMMY. I certainly has. I stuck right here guarding the old place all the time.

CROSBY. Haven't you been lonely—living here by yourself?

MAMMY. No, sir. I've got my friends.

CROSBY. Friends!

MAMMY. Yes, my friends from the shadow world!

CROSBY. (*Cynically*) Oh! *You* believe in spirits, eh?

5

MAMMY. I don't believe. I know. They are with me all the time —— (*She makes a mysterious gesture in the air.*)

CROSBY. (*Amused*) You never really saw one, did you, Mammy?

MAMMY. (*Coming to him, her eyes bright with feverish excitement*) Yes, sir—I see 'em! And they done warn me there's a evil spirit working around this house.

CROSBY. (*Amused*) Ever see it?

MAMMY. No, sir—but I felt it—pass me in the dark—on the stairs ——

CROSBY. (*At safe*) Nonsense, your nerves are upset—it's living alone—here all this time ——

MAMMY. No, sir!

CROSBY. (*Working combination at safe*) Never mind, cheer up! In a few minutes the house will be full of people, and all your spooks will vanish.

MAMMY. How many heirs coming?

CROSBY. Six! All the surviving relatives. By the way—Mammy—your job as guardian of this house is up to-night. What are you going to do? (*Opens safe and takes out will.*)

MAMMY. It all depends. If I like the new heirs —I stay here. If I don't—I goes back to the West Indies.

(CROSBY *closes safe in wall and moves to front of sofa.*)

CROSBY. There's the will. It's been in that safe, undisturbed for the last twenty years, think of that. (*In front of sofa.*)

MAMMY. (*Looking at him sardonically*) I'se thinking.

CROSBY. (*Opens portfolio and takes out three large sealed envelopes*) There you are, just as your master sealed them, and locked them in that safe—

marked one, two, three—hello. (*As he is looking at them he shows excitement. He examines each seal intently.*) These envelopes have been opened —every one of them! The seals have been cut away and very cleverly glued back again. Someone has opened that safe and read this will.

MAMMY. How could they? Nobody knows how to open the safe but you.

CROSBY. (*With anger*) Well, I didn't do it.

MAMMY. I ain't suspecting nobody—I'd just like to know—why they opened 'em. (*Grins at him venomously.*) What you expect they'd want to do, change the will?

CROSBY. (*Looking at her keenly*) Perhaps. But if it *has* been changed, it won't do them any good. I drew up duplicate wills, according to Mr. West's instructions. One copy is here—the other is in the vault of the Empire Trust Company and if this one *has* been tampered with, I'll know it— and I'll know who did it. (*Door-bell rings.*)

MAMMY. You don't think that I ——

CROSBY. See who that is, Mammy. And mind —say nothing about this.

(MAMMY *gives him a poisonous look and exits.* CROSBY *starts looking for a secret spring near bookcase up* R. *and stops as he hears* MAMMY *at door.* MAMMY *opens door, admits* HARRY BLYTHE, *a tall, dark man about thirty-five years of age. A quiet, cynical, bored man, but dangerous. He is of the gentleman heavy type.*)

HARRY. (*Enters, shakes hands with* CROSBY) How are you, Mr. Crosby?

CROSBY. Hello, Harry! Did you come up on the train?

HARRY. No. Some friends of mine motored me

over from Tarrytown. The train had just pulled in as I passed the station. Am I the first of the pack?

CROSBY. Yes. I guess the others will be right up.

HARRY. How many heirs besides myself?

CROSBY. Five.

HARRY. Five, eh? Well, I'm fortunate. I only know two of them, and I wish to heaven I only knew one.

CROSBY. (*Slowly*) Why do you dislike Charlie Wilder?

HARRY. In the first place because he is my cousin, in the second place because he's a poet, and —— (*Lights cigarette.*)

CROSBY. (*Grins*) And in the third place, because Annabelle is very fond of him!

HARRY. You've said it! (*Looks at him, then turns away and changes subject.*) So this is the old man's library?

CROSBY. Yes. Haven't you ever been here before?

HARRY. No. Why did you ask?

CROSBY. (*Glancing at will in his hand*) Well, someone has.

HARRY. (*Quickly*) Just what do you mean by that?

CROSBY. (*Turning away*) Oh, nothing.

HARRY. (*Sees* MAMMY *in doorway*) I beg your pardon, would you mind parking yourself in the kitchen for a while?

(MAMMY *glares at him venomously, but at a nod from* CROSBY, *exits.*)

CROSBY. You've offended her. Do you know who she is?

HARRY. (*Coming* C.) No.

CROSBY. She's Mr. West's old and trusted servant.

HARRY. That's possibly all very true—but it's not interesting. What are you getting at?

CROSBY. You mustn't treat her like an ordinary servant. She's a West Indian—a voodoo woman.

HARRY. (*Smiles*) My dear fellow—I don't care what she is. Is that the will?

CROSBY. (*Offended by his manner*) Yes, but it can't be read until all the heirs are assembled in this room. (*Crosses to safe and closes panel.*)

HARRY. (*Seated on arm of chair*) All right. Oh, Mr. Crosby. You knew old man West—was he all there?

CROSBY. *All* there?

HARRY. Wasn't he a little bit off? You know, a little coo-coo. Didn't he collect things—in the West Indies?

CROSBY. (*Sternly*) Have you no respect for a dead relative?

HARRY. (*Cheerfully*) None whatever—unless, of course, he has made me the sole heir. (*Laughs and sits down to read a book.*) Come on, Mr. Crosby—you'll admit he was a nut.

CROSBY. (*Slowly*) He was a little eccentric.

HARRY. Eccentric! He was fantastic! Why did he want a twenty-year-old will read to his heirs —at midnight in this old house? Why not in the daytime at your office? Why drag us out here?

CROSBY. (*Coming in front of sofa*) Mr. West stipulated—that this will should be read—in this room—at the very hour of his death—one of his whims. (*Crosses C. to back of table L.*)

HARRY. Whim —— (*Rises.*) It's going to make me miss the last train to New York and I'll have to sleep here.

CROSBY. That's all been taken care of. (*Goes to* HARRY R. C.) Mammy will see that you're made comfortable, and you'll have company—the others will have to sleep here, too. (MAMMY *opens door and admits two more heirs,* CICILY YOUNG, *a pretty blond girl and* SUSAN SILLSBY, *a female with an acid temper. Seeing* SUSAN.) How do you do!

SUSAN. How do you do!

CROSBY. (*Shakes hands with* CICILY) You two know each other?

SUSAN. Oh, yes, yes—we met after we got off the train. My, what a small world it is.

CICILY. I overheard Miss Sillsby asking for a taxi to take her to Glencliff, so we rode up together.

SUSAN. What was I saying? Oh, yes—I was telling Cicily ——

CROSBY. Excuse me, Miss Sillsby—let me introduce Mr. Harry Blythe. Miss Susan Sillsby and Miss Cicily Young ——

HARRY. Ladies, delighted!

SUSAN. (*Gushes over to* HARRY) So you are Harry Blythe! Well! Well! Well! My, what a small world it is.

HARRY. Yes, isn't it?

SUSAN. (*Taking* HARRY *by the arm to front of sofa*) Now, you must tell me all about yourself. We must find out just how we're connected! Did you know my Great-aunt Eleanor ——

HARRY. (*Interrupting*) No, Miss Sillsby, I did not know your Great-aunt Eleanor.

SUSAN. Well, she's ——

HARRY. I'm not anxious to hear about her—so why delve into ancient history?

SUSAN. But I ——

HARRY. Aunt Eleanor and I are related—aren't we?

SUSAN. Yes ——

HARRY. It can't be helped ——

SUSAN. No!

HARRY. So let it go at that. (*Crosses* R. *of table* R.)

SUSAN. (*Bounces back to* CICILY) Why—he's the rudest man I ever met—he's positively insulting!

CICILY. Don't pay any attention to him. He doesn't know any better probably. Anyway, I like him better than I do this house. (*Looks around.*) It's such a spooky old place!

SUSAN. You know, my dear—I've had the queerest feeling ever since we came in the house. I feel as if someone were—peering at me —— Oh! (*Suddenly sees* MAMMY *looking fixedly at her.*) This house is haunted. I know it.

MAMMY. (*Keeping her eyes on* SUSAN, *speaks in a deep sepulchral voice*) Lady, there is someone in the other world trying to tell you something. You is mediumistic—(*Cry from* SUSAN.) a spiritist —I knew it when you came in that door. There are spirits all around you.

SUSAN. (*Sits chair* C.) I knew it—I knew it.

CROSBY. (*Sternly*) What are you trying to do, Mammy? Frighten her to death?

HARRY. (*Laughs*) Nonsense—(*To end of sofa.*) no one was ever frightened to death.

CROSBY. It has happened, and you know it. Lots of women have lost their minds—sometimes their lives—through—fright. The asylums are full of such cases. (MAMMY *exits.*)

HARRY. (CROSBY *walks down* L. *in front of table*) I don't believe it ——

SUSAN. (*Rises*) Oh, I wish I hadn't come— you heard what she said! It's terrible—I want to go home. (CICILY *takes her over to sofa.*)

HARRY. Come and sit down.

SUSAN. I don't want to sit down. (*Sits on sofa.*)

(MAMMY *opens door and admits* CHARLIE WILDER. CHARLIE *is a tall, handsome, leading man type*

He is full of charm—smiles all the time, and has a magnetic personality. CHARLIE *down to* CROSBY.)

CHARLIE. (*Holding out his hand to* CROSBY) How are you, Mr. Crosby? Hope I'm not late. (*Looks toward the ladies.*)

CROSBY. Hello, Charlie! Miss Susan Sillsby and Miss Cicily Young—this is Charlie Wilder, another distant relative.

CHARLIE. (*Smiles and shakes hands with them*) It's a pleasure to discover that I have such charming relatives.

SUSAN. Oh!

CROSBY. Oh, Harry, you know Charlie, of course ——

HARRY. (*Coming* C.—*stands, staring at* CHARLIE) Oh, yes, I know him!

CROSBY. Now, boys, forget this foolish quarrel of yours. This is a family reunion—stop acting like children and shake hands.

CHARLIE. I'd like to. Come on, old man. Let's bury the hatchet. Shake! (*Offers hand to* HARRY. HARRY *shakes hands reluctantly. Drops his hand, turns to* CROSBY.) When are you going to read the will, Mr. Crosby?

CROSBY. As soon as the other two heirs arrive. (*'Phone.*) Excuse me. (*Sits* L. *of table. Answers telephone.*) Hello—yes—yes, this is Mr. Crosby. (*Listens.*) Oh, all right—yes, we're waiting for you. (*Hangs up 'phone.*) That's one of them now. She's on her way from the station. She had trouble getting a taxi.

CHARLIE. (*Back of table*) I left the other downstairs. Chap by the name of Jones.

CROSBY. What's he doing down there?

CHARLIE.   Arguing with the driver of the taxi we came up in.

(MAMMY *admits* PAUL JONES.)

CROSBY.   (*Holds out his hand*)   Come in, Paul. Glad to see you.   My, my, but you're looking fit!

PAUL.   (*Shaking hands with him doubtfully*) Well, I may look all right—but I don't feel so good ——

CROSBY.   No ——

PAUL.   I have felt better—but on the other hand, I *have* felt worse.

CROSBY.   Here are some cousins you ought to know, Miss Cicily Young.   Mr. Paul Jones.

CICILY.   (*Seated* L. *of sofa.   Smiles*)   So you're Cousin Paul ——

PAUL.   Yep!   That's who it is.

CICILY.   Isn't it a wonderful night?

PAUL.   Well, the sky didn't look any too good when I came in but of course on the other hand it may be all right by to-morrow.

CROSBY.   Miss Sillsby, Mr. Jones.

SUSAN.   (*Crosses to* PAUL, *gushing*)   Well! Well!   Paul Jones?

PAUL.   Yep!

SUSAN.   Isn't the world a small place?

PAUL.   Yep, it certainly is but not too small.

SUSAN.   I quite agree with you.   You're a professional man, aren't you?

PAUL.   Yes, ma'am, *I'm* a horse doctor.

(SUSAN *crosses to sofa and sits.*)

CHARLIE.   (*Coming around the* R. *of* PAUL) Horse doctor!

CROSBY.   Oh, Paul, your cousin Charlie Wilder ——

CHARLIE.   How do you do!

CROSBY.   And Harry Blythe ——

PAUL.   Mr. Blythe!

CHARLIE.   I thought you were in the automobile business.

PAUL.   Well, when I graduated from college as a first-class vet, I went back home to practice and found I was sunk.   The farmers had quit using horses and were all driving cars, so I naturally began doctoring them—there isn't much difference, is there—and I want to tell you I've got about the snappiest garage in Wickford.

MAMMY.   (*Who has been in the door all this time, suddenly speaks*)   I hear a taxi comin' down the drive—the sixth heir.   (MAMMY *looks at them with a malicious smile and exits.*)

CICILY.   (*Shows fear*)   Ugh!   She gives me the creeps.

CHARLIE.   (*Up to door*)   She is rather weird. I don't hear any taxi.

SUSAN.   This house is haunted.

PAUL.   (*With a start*)   Eh!

SUSAN.   I know it!

CROSBY.   Rubbish!   (*Turns to* SUSAN.)   You'll be seeing ghosts the first thing you know.

PAUL.   (*Nervously*)   Well, personally, I've never seen a ghost—however, on the other hand, that doesn't prove that there aren't any.   I've felt kinda queer ever since I've been in this house.

HARRY.   What will you do with it if you inherit it?

PAUL.   I don't expect to inherit it.   I never (*Crossing to* HARRY L.) inherit anything—but on the other hand you never can tell, I might.

(MAMMY *opens door and* ANNABELLE WEST *enters.* ANNABELLE *is a vigorous, beautiful girl, frank and fearless and very modern.*)

ANNABELLE. Sorry I'm late, Mr. Crosby.
CROSBY. (*Greets her*) Well, Annabelle, you did get here. Miss Cicily Young—Miss Annabelle West.

(ANNABELLE *smiles and shakes hands with them.*)

CICILY. Annabelle West, the illustrator?
ANNA. I suppose so!
CROSBY. Miss Sillsby, Miss West.
HARRY. (*To* C.) Hello, Annabelle!

(*As* ANNABELLE *turns and sees* HARRY, *she gasps in amazement.*)

ANNA. Harry!
CHARLIE. (*Coming down* C.) Annabelle!

(*Then seeing* CHARLIE, ANNABELLE *gasps in great amazement.*)

ANNA. Charlie Wilder! Why didn't I see you on the train?
CHARLIE. I was in the smoker.
HARRY. I motored up. Now you can go ahead, Mr. Crosby.

(ANNABELLE *is speechless for a moment.*)

CROSBY. (L. *of table*) If you'll all sit down, I'll begin.
CHARLIE. Annabelle! (CHARLIE *offers chair at* R. *of table which* ANNABELLE *takes. At the same time,* HARRY *pushes armchair for* ANNABELLE *to sit in and* PAUL *takes it.*)
ANNA. (*As she sits down, she sees* PAUL *staring at her with open mouth*) Well, Cousin Paul?
PAUL. (*Who has been staring at her, fascinated,*

with his mouth wide open, chokes and stammers) Yes, that's right. Little Annabelle West—all growed up an' everything.

ANNA. *(Smiles and takes his hand)* When did you leave Wickford?

PAUL. This morning, I think—yes, as a matter of fact I ——

CROSBY. *(Is seated)* Now I'm going to be brief.

HARRY. *(Flippantly)* Good!

(PAUL *gives him a look.*)

CROSBY. *(Glares at him)* Cyrus Canby West died in this house twenty years ago to-night. He made me executor of his estate. Mr. West was a very eccentric man—and hated all his living relatives.

HARRY. *(Sotto voce)* I don't blame him.

CROSBY. Not wishing his near relatives to enjoy his fortune, Mr. West invested it in Government bonds to mature in twenty years. At the end of that time I was to assemble all his surviving relatives and read his will. Now you understand why I've kept track of you all. You six people are the last living descendants of Cyrus Canby West.

HARRY. I thought you were going to make this brief.

CROSBY. Please! *(Holds up the three envelopes.)* Here is the will in these three envelopes.
                                          (GONG.)
(At this moment, a muffled, weird gong sounds somewhere in the house. It tolls seven and stops. GONG seven strokes.) I will now read instructions on envelope marked 1.

(Everyone looks at each other with a certain amount of nervousness.)

MAMMY. (*In trance*) Oh, tell me—oh, tell me!

(*Everyone turns and looks at* MAMMY.)

CROSBY. (*Annoyed, because in spite of himself he is chilled by the unearthly gong, turns to* MAMMY) Mammy—Mammy Pleasant!

MAMMY. (*Who has been standing near the door, has her eyes closed, and is rocking her body to and fro, muttering incantations to herself*) Yes—I hear you—Eliza ——

CROSBY. Mammy!

MAMMY. Eliza, what are you trying to tell me about—about ——

CROSBY. (*Sharply*) Mammy! Stop that and answer me.

MAMMY. Tell me—tell me the name ——

CROSBY. (*Sharply*) Mammy!

MAMMY. (*Opening eyes*) What?

CROSBY. What was that noise—like a gong?

MAMMY. (*In a deep voice surcharged with malice*) That is the warning of death. The master heard it just before *he* died.

(*All look at each other impressed in spite of themselves.* PAUL *stands up and mops his brow with his handkerchief and runs his hand around his collar, which has suddenly grown too tight.*)

PAUL. I've been thinking that there isn't any use of my staying round here, besides, I don't feel so good—and it looks like rain, so if it's all the same to you, I think I'll run to the station. (*Starts for the door.* MAMMY *moves in front of him.*)

ANNA. (*Stops him and begins to laugh*) Nonsense, Paul, it isn't going to rain—and I want you here to—to —— You don't believe in ghosts, do you?

PAUL. No! No! Of course not! But then on the other hand that gong and ——

CROSBY. It's nothing ——

ANNA. An old grandfather's clock in one of the rooms.

MAMMY. There is no clock running in this house.

PAUL. You see!

MAMMY. The toll says seven may live. There is eight persons in this room. One must die before morning.

SUSAN. Oh! I feel faint.

PAUL. Say, listen, honest to goodness, it's too hot in here. I want some air. (PAUL *starts for door.* HARRY *grabs* PAUL *and forces him in chair.*)

HARRY. Quit your kidding and sit down.

PAUL. (*As he sits down*) But I'm not kidding.

HARRY. Crosby, go on with the will.

CROSBY. (*Clears his throat, and reads instructions on envelope 1*) "At midnight, September 27, 1921, you will open this envelope and read its contents to such of my relatives (*Movement of everybody.*) as are assembled in my library at Glencliff Manor." (*He opens the envelope, takes out sheet of paper and reads.*) "First, let my executor ask the prospective heirs assembled this night if they are willing to take what fortune offers them, and not question my judgment in the manner in which I shall dispose of my fortune." (*He looks up inquiringly.*) Is that clear? Any objections?

SUSAN. No, that's all right, go ahead.

(*All nod satisfaction.*)

CROSBY. "If they are willing ——"

PAUL. Just a minute, I don't know about that.

Maybe his judgment isn't good. Mind you, I don't say that it isn't, but then on the other hand it might not be.

CROSBY. Are you satisfied or not?

PAUL. Well, it seems to me under the circumstances ——

CHARLIE. Sure he is—go on.

CROSBY. Are you?

PAUL. I didn't say I wasn't. I merely started to say that it seemed to me under the circumstances ——

HARRY. Will you dry up?

CROSBY. (*Continues reading*) " If they are willing to take what fortune offers, then let my executor open envelope number two and read my will." (*He puts down the paper, opens the envelope marked 2. All show their anxiety and lean forward to hear as he reads.*) " I, Cyrus Canby West, being of sound mind and body, do hereby declare as the sole heir to all my money, bonds, securities, estate, real and otherwise, my descendant, man or woman who bears the surname of West. If more than one bear the surname of West, then my estate shall be equally divided among them. Cyrus Canby West. Witnesses: Mammy Pleasant, Roger Crosby." (CROSBY *looks up and pauses.* PAUL *stands up to congratulate* ANNABELLE.) There is, however, a codicil. (PAUL *coughs and sits.* CROSBY *continues to read.*) " In the event of the death of the beneficiary, or if he or she be proved of unsound mind, or if it be proved in a court of law that the said beneficiary is not competent to properly handle the estate, then my executor will open envelope marked 3 and declare the next heir." (CROSBY *puts down paper, looks at them and speaks.*) Therefore—(*Rises.*) in accordance with the will. I now declare Miss Annabelle West as sole heiress of the West estate, and the mistress of

Glencliff Manor. Annabelle, I congratulate you. (*Offers his hand.* PAUL *rises—moves chair back.*) And as there is no doubt as to the good health and sanity of Miss West—I trust this envelope shall never be opened. (*Puts envelope in his pocket.*)

CHARLIE. (*Over table*) It's wonderful, Annabelle, I'm glad.

HARRY. I congratulate you with all my heart. (*Crosses to back of chair* C.)

ANNA. (*Dazed by her good fortune*) I—I can't realize it yet—all I can say is—that Glencliff is open to you all—and everything I have is —— (*Almost breaks down.*)

SUSAN. (*On sofa*) I knew there was a catch in it.

CICILY. (*Rises, crosses and shakes hands*) I confess I'm disappointed, but I congratulate you.

ANNA. Thanks.

(CICILY *crosses up to* L. *of* HARRY.)

SUSAN. (*With an acid smile*) I suppose there's nothing else to do, but to wish you many happy returns.

ANNA. It is so—so unexpected—I can hardly —— (*Turns to* CROSBY.) I can't believe it yet. (*To* PAUL.) Isn't it wonderful?

PAUL. (L. *of sofa*) Well, of course, money doesn't always bring happiness—but then again on the other hand, sometimes it does.

SUSAN. I quite agree with you, money is the root of all evil.

PAUL. It is, it certainly is! When you haven't got any! (*Goes up stage.*)

ANNA. (*To* CROSBY) Mr. Crosby, one thing puzzles me about the will.

CROSBY. What is it?

ANNA. What did he mean when it said if the heir is proved to be unsound in mind?

CROSBY. Mr. West believed that there was a streak of insanity in the family. That clause was put there in case that failing should reappear in the heir. In that event, the estate would go to the heir named in envelope three.

(ANNABELLE *sits* R. *of table.* CROSBY *sits* L. *of table.*)

PAUL. I wonder who that is?

HARRY. I wonder.

ANNA. I didn't know there was any insanity in our family.

HARRY. Neither did I until I heard that will.

CROSBY. But it is legal—absolutely!

HARRY. I don't dispute that—I'm only saying that the old man was doty.

CROSBY. He was peculiar, yes, but as sane as any man living.

MAMMY. (*Comes to* R. *of* ANNABELLE *and offers her a ring full of keys*) Here are the keys to the house, Miss West.

ANNA. Won't you remain as my housekeeper?

MAMMY. (*Puts keys in pocket of apron. She takes out a sealed envelope, hands it to* ANNABELLE) When Mr. West died he gave me this letter to give to the heir after the will was read. (MAMMY *backs up to door again.*)

ANNA. (*Reads what is written on the outside of the envelope*) "You will open this envelope tonight, in my room, where you are to sleep." (*Looks at* CROSBY, *then puts the letter in her pocket.*) Where is the room, Mammy?

MAMMY. (*Points*) There. Across the hall.

CICILY. (*To* HARRY) I agree with you. Mr. West was certainly insane. Imagine trusting that woman to deliver a letter twenty years after his death.

CROSBY. (*Blankly*) It's all news to me. Mammy, when did he give you that letter?

MAMMY. Just before he died, when you and the doctor were talking in a corner of the room. (*Glaring at* CICILY.)

SUSAN. I'm afraid that Cousin Cyrus *was* a little out of his mind.

PAUL. (*To* SUSAN) I wonder what's in that letter.

CROSBY. It may refer to the lost necklace.

HARRY. Necklace?

CICILY. (*Coming down* C. *To* HARRY) Oh, I remember my mother telling me she saw it once and said it was the most gorgeous thing imaginable. All sapphires and rubies.

ANNA. Seems to me I heard something about it. (*To* CROSBY.) Wasn't it a family heirloom?

CICILY. Yes. Mother told me it had been in the family for—oh, generations. But she said it was lost or stolen—after it came into Mr. West's possession.

CROSBY. It did disappear—but I don't think it was lost or stolen. I believe Mr. West hid it—somewhere in this house.

CHARLIE. Why should he do that?

CROSBY. Another of his whims.

SUSAN. Did you ever see it?

CROSBY. Once. It was magnificent. The stones alone are worth a fortune. Annabelle, I congratulate you again.

SUSAN. (PAUL *goes up* R.) Gracious—some people have all the luck.

CICILY. You know the old saying—" Them that has—gets."

ANNA. (*Excited*) Before I go to bed (*Rises.*) ll open this letter. Perhaps in the morning I will show you the necklace. This is going to be a wonderful evening. Mammy, how about some supper?

MAMMY. I'll put it on the table in the dining-room.

ANNA. While you're doing that, we'll explore the place—and you two can pick out your rooms.

CICILY. I'd like one next to Susan. I'm afraid to sleep alone in this ghostly old house.

SUSAN. (*Crosses to* CICILY) I know I won't sleep a wink.

ANNA. Nonsense. There is nothing to fear.

CICILY. Aren't you afraid to sleep in the room where he died?

ANNA. Certainly not, why should I be?

SUSAN. (*Exaggerated*) This house is haunted, she—(*Points to* MAMMY.) has seen them—spirits!

ANNA. Suppose she has? She has been living here a long time—and they haven't hurt you, have they?

MAMMY. (*At door*) But there is an evil spirit in this house now ——

ANNA. (*Just a trifle nervous*) I don't believe it—nothing can frighten me.

CHARLIE. (*Seeing that* ANNABELLE *is growing nervous*) Keep still! Don't you see—you are making Miss West nervous.

(MAMMY *gives a venomous look and goes out.*)

ANNA. (*Starting after* MAMMY—L. *of door*) Come on, Susan and Cicily ——

SUSAN. I won't budge without a man.

ANNA. Come on, Paul, you'll protect us, won't you?

PAUL. (*Going toward door*) Well, I don't know as I'd be much use to you—but then again, on the other hand, you never can tell—maybe I might. (*Exits with* ANNABELLE.)

(SUSAN *moves up stage.*)

CICILY. (R. C., *speaking at* CROSBY) I haven't much confidence in Paul—I wish Mr. Crosby would come!

CROSBY. Me?—I—of course I'll come—delighted.

SUSAN. The more the merrier ——

(*Exeunt* CICILY *and* SUSAN.)

CROSBY. (*At door. To* HARRY *and* CHARLIE) Why don't you boys make it up! (*Exits, and closes door.*)

CHARLIE. (*As soon as they are alone, he grins at* HARRY *and crosses to* C.) Here we are again!

HARRY. (*Coming over to* CHARLIE) But it won't be for long. One of us will be gone before morning ——

CHARLIE. Meaning me?

HARRY. You!

CHARLIE. Until *Annabelle* tells me I'm not wanted, I'm going to stick right here.

HARRY. You won't stick here and you won't get her—except —— Well, just try it!

CHARLIE. Now that she's the heiress, you've decided that you're in love with her.

HARRY. I've decided that she needs my protection—(ANNABELLE *reënters.*) and she's going to have it.—So you keep out of my way—or I'll —— (HARRY *makes a threatening move.*)

ANNA. Well—what's it all about?

HARRY. Nothing! (*Turns away to back of sofa.* CHARLIE *moves over to table* L.)

CHARLIE. Sorry to disappoint you, Annabelle. Where did you put me?

ANNA. At the end of the hall. Mammy will show you. Harry, you are to sleep in the first room at the head of the stairs.

CHARLIE. Find any spirits in the house?

ANNA. The sideboard is full of Scotch whiskey. Run along—make yourself a highball!

CHARLIE. (*Going to door*) All right, I will, but I'd like to see you later, Annabelle.

ANNA. Come back when you've had your Scotch.

CHARLIE. I will. And I'll bring you some. (CHARLIE *exits, closes door.*)

ANNA. (*To sofa*) Harry, what's all this nonsense between you and Charlie?

HARRY. It isn't nonsense, Annabelle. It's serious. You know how I—think about you, and it exasperates me the way you smile on that rotter.

ANNA. See here, Harry, don't talk that way about Charlie—he's one of my dearest friends

HARRY. If he's a sample of your dearest friends, God help you!

ANNA. I used to think you were one of them, but when I see you with such an ugly look in your eyes —— (*Sits.*)

HARRY. You're shocked, are you?

ANNA. No! I've *always* thought there was a good deal of the brute in you ——

HARRY. And is that why you told me to run along and find some other girl?

ANNA. Not exactly. I didn't mind the brute in you—I was only afraid you mightn't be able to control it—and it looks as though I were right.

HARRY. How can a man control himself when he sees the woman he loves is being swept off her feet by a romantic milksop?

ANNA. (*Rises*) If you mean Charlie ——

HARRY. I do. (*She goes* L. *He follows.*)

Charlie's a dreamer—a visionary. He'll never amount to a row of pins. Don't throw yourself away on him!   .

ANNA. Do you suggest that I throw myself away on you?

HARRY. You'd better!

ANNA. Is that a threat?

HARRY. Whatever it is, Annabelle—it comes straight from my heart.

ANNA. Just for a moment—the old trust in you —comes back to me.

HARRY. And if you'll give me the chance I'll make you trust me forever.

ANNA. It's too late.

HARRY. You love him ——

ANNA. (*Crosses in front of table*) Please!

HARRY. All right, but I know a cure for it!

ANNA. A cure?

HARRY. Yes! Just marry him! . . . And you can take my word for it, you'll be sorry as long as you live.

ANNA. (*Lightly*) What are you doing—putting a curse on me?

HARRY. What do you want me to do—give you my blessing?

ANNA. You can give me one thing—a promise— (*Crosses to* HARRY. *Holds out her hand.*) that you'll always be my friend.

HARRY. (*Taking her hand*) That goes! You'll need me, Annabelle, and when you do, I'll come a-running.

ANNABELLE. I've a mind to give you a kiss for that!

HARRY. No, thanks—I want all or none.

(*Enter* CROSBY, *followed by* CHARLIE, *who brings on tray, whiskey bottle and glasses.*)

CROSBY.   Annabelle, as hostess, I think you might hurry along the supper.

ANNA.   (*Starting for door*)   Mammy may not like my interfering but I'll see what I can do. (*Exits.*)

CROSBY.   (*To CHARLIE*)   That was a great highball! Charlie! Just like old times.

CHARLIE.   I'll say the old man knew Scotch.

HARRY.   I'll say he didn't know much about wills.

(SUSAN *enters in trance—she stands staring into space.* PAUL *reënters.*)

SUSAN.   I know it—I know it, I know it.   (*In front of chair* R. *of table.*)

PAUL.   (*Uneasy—to* CROSBY)   What's—what's the matter with her?

CROSBY.   (*To* SUSAN)   Anything wrong, Miss Sillsby?

SUSAN.   I know it, just as sure as I'm standing on this spot.

PAUL.   What do you know?

SUSAN.   That something is going to happen. Something terrible.   (HARRY *laughs.*)   Don't you laugh at me, Harry Blythe. Don't you know Aunt Eleanor is trying to warn me?

PAUL.   What's she trying to warn you about?

SUSAN.   Some danger.   (PAUL *crosses to sofa.*)

HARRY.   (*Coming down* L. *of sofa*)   Miss Sillsby, aren't you stretching your imagination— just a little?

CHARLIE.   (*Back of table*)   You're not a medium, are you?

SUSAN.   Yes. I've always thought I was a psychic, and now I know it. Didn't you hear Mammy Pleasant say a spirit was trying to warn me? **Aunt Eleanor!**

CROSBY. (*Indulgently*) You mustn't believe everything that Mammy tells you, Miss Sillsby.

SUSAN. But I do. I felt it in my bones, the moment I entered this house, that something terrible was going to happen. (*Crosses to* L. *of sofa.*)

PAUL. (*On sofa*) And I suppose if nothing terrible happens—you'll be disappointed?

(MAMMY *starts to open door.*)

SUSAN. (*Acidly*) Mr. Jones! Really!

PAUL. Sorry—no offense.

MAMMY. (*Opens door*) There's a man outside. He says he wants to see the boss of this house.

CROSBY. Who is he?

MAMMY. He's from the sanitarium at Fairview.

CROSBY. You mean—the asylum?

MAMMY. Yes, sir.

CROSBY. What does he want?

MAMMY. I don't know.

(CROSBY *looks at the others, perplexed.*)

HARRY. Why not see him, and find out?

CROSBY. Send him in, Mammy.

(MAMMY *exits and closes door.* SUSAN *sits chair* C.)

CHARLIE. (*Lights cigarette*) Could he be after some ——

HARRY. Where is this asylum, Mr. Crosby?

CROSBY. Up past the village. (*Looks at all of them.*) What do you suppose he wants?

PAUL. Maybe he wants to take one of us back with him.

(MAMMY *admits* HENDRICKS, *a typical guard— rough and brutal, with a dangerous manner. He carries a straight jacket.*)

MAMMY. This is the man.

HENDRICKS. (*Looks at* CHARLIE, *then* HARRY, *then* MAMMY, *who exits and closes door. He then comes* C. *to* CROSBY) Are you the boss?

CROSBY. I represent the owner of this house. Who are you?

HENDRICKS. My name's Hendricks. I'm the head guard up at Fairview.

CROSBY. Yes, I know. What are you doing down here?

HENDRICKS. We're looking for a patient who got away this afternoon. (*Crosses to window below table.*)

CHARLIE. A patient!

HARRY. You mean you're looking for an escaped lunatic?

HENDRICKS. (*Looks at* HARRY) Yes.

HARRY. Why didn't you come right out with it?

HENDRICKS. (*Gruffly*) Because I didn't want to scare you.

CROSBY. (*Quickly*) Is there any cause for alarm?

HENDRICKS. Yes.

CROSBY. And this—this patient is dangerous?

HENDRICKS. (*Crosses to* CROSBY) Dangerous! (*Pauses.*) He's a killer. A homicidal maniac!

CHARLIE. (*Sharply*) What makes you think he's here?

HENDRICKS. (*In a surly tone to* CHARLIE) I didn't say he was here. I'm asking at all the houses, and thought I was doing a favor in warning you, that's all.

CROSBY. (*Placating him*) Just a minute. No offense was intended.

HENDRICKS. (*Stops and turns*) Well?

CROSBY. Have you any reason to believe he might be around here?

HENDRICKS. (*Comes down a step*) Well, he

might be in any of these houses. You see, he always gets in a house when he escapes, and hides until everyone goes to bed—then he prowls around like ——

HARRY. He's escaped before?

HENDRICKS. Yes. He got away from us about a year ago, and hid in a house in the village, and—well, I got there just in time.

HARRY. What does he look like?

HENDRICKS. When he escaped he had on a black slouch hat and a long coat. He's an old guy, with a bald head, sharp teeth and finger-nails—like claws. He crawls around on all fours like a ——

CROSBY. An animal?

HENDRICXS. Yeh, a cat!

HARRY. A cat!

HENDRICKS. Yes, and I'm the only one up there that can handle him. (*Grins at them brutally.*) He's afraid of me.

CHARLIE. (*With irony*) I suppose you control him through kindness.

HENDRICKS. (*With a savage laugh*) Control him through kindness! Yes, I do—not. I control him with a club, a chair, an iron bar—anything I can get my hands on. (*To others.*) We have to keep him strapped down most of the time in this straight jacket! (*Shows it.*)

CHARLIE. That's the cruelest thing I ever heard of. Think of being strapped down in that—it's enough to make anyone violent.

HENDRICKS. (*Sneeringly*) You don't say so. Hah!

CHARLIE. Yes, and I dare say, because of his treatment up there, this old man thinks everyone is against him. He's probably just a poor old nut.

HENDRICKS. (*To* CHARLIE *with a truculent air*) Poor old nut! Say, young feller, let me tell you. this poor old nut could rip you wide open—just like a cat rips open a bird. Don't make any mistake about him. (*To others.*)   The last time I got him he had his hands —— (*Indicates strangling.*) Well, it took three of us to get him away. (*Looks at all of them and then sneers at* CHARLIE.)   Poor old nut! Say, young feller, you take my tip, if you see him—you—you run like hell!

SUSAN. (*Gasps with terror*) Oh!

HENDRICKS.   Sorry, ma'am, I forgot you was there. (*Crosses to window in front of table.*)

SUSAN.   Do you think ——

HENDRICKS.   Now don't get excited. It ain't likely he's around here. (*Comes back to* C.)

CROSBY.   Where are the rest of your men?

HENDRICKS.   Looking over the estate—next to this one. (*Goes to door.*)   Well, I guess I'll be going.

CROSBY.   But suppose ——

HENDRICKS. (*Coming down*) Don't get nervous, he ain't liable to ever get in this house. 'Tain't likely he's even around here.

CROSBY. (*Relieved*) You think so?

HENDRICKS.   Sure. He may be prowling around the neighborhood, waiting for a chance to sneak in somewhere, so just to play safe, none of you had better go out before morning. (*Pauses a moment and speaks seriously.*)   But—be sure to lock all the outside doors and windows. I'll be around here, and if we get him, I'll drop in and let you know— good-night. (*Exits.*)

CROSBY. (*Pauses—turning to them all*) What do you think we ought to do?

CHARLIE. (*To everyone*) We'd better not say anything about this to Annabelle or Cicily. It would only throw them into a panic.

HARRY. (*Insolently*) You're wrong. Both these girls should be told. If there *is* any danger they ought to know it.

CHARLIE. What do you think, Mr. Crosby?

CROSBY. I agree with *you*. It would throw them into a panic. I don't believe there is any danger, so there is no use alarming them. Harry, you won't tell them, will you?

HARRY. I don't know about that —— (*Turns to* PAUL.) What do you think, Paul?

PAUL. I think I'd better go down and lock all the cellar windows.

SUSAN. Yes! Yes! Do, do!

(HARRY *touches* PAUL *on shoulder.* PAUL *jumps with exclamation.*)

PAUL. Oh!

HARRY. I mean about telling the girls.

PAUL. (*Doubtfully*) Well, I don't know. Maybe they ought to be told and on the other hand maybe they oughtn't.

HARRY. (*Back of sofa*) You're a lot of help to me! (*To* CROSBY.) You win. I shall say nothing

CROSBY. (*To* PAUL) You'll keep quiet, Paul?

PAUL. (*Doubtfully*) Well, I don't know—it seems to me under the circumstances ——

CROSBY. (*Exasperated*) Will you answer me?

PAUL. What I started to say was—it seems to me under the circumstances ——

CROSBY. Will you or won't you?

PAUL. (*Rises*) Well, you don't give me a chance to talk —— (*Rises.*) Of course I won't say anything. (*Goes back of sofa to bookcase.*)

CROSBY. Now, Susan, promise not to mention this to the girls!

SUSAN. Of course I won't. Good heavens, do you think I'm the kind who can't keep a secret? (*Rises.*) Let me tell you, Mr. Crosby, that we girls don't talk half as much as you men. (CROSBY *goes to window.* SUSAN *changes her voice to a moan.*)   Oh dear—oh dear—I just know we'll all be murdered in our beds. (*Crosses to sofa.*)

HARRY.   (*Grins*)   Cheer up—the worst is yet to come.   (*Cautions silence as* CICILY *enters and leaves door open.*)

CICILY.   Annabelle wants you to come to supper!

CROSBY.   We'll be right along.

CICILY.   (*Goes to* SUSAN *on couch*)   Why, Cousin Sue—what is it?

SUSAN.   (*Getting up*)   Oh, it's nothing—nothing!   Come, Cicily, I must have a strong cup of tea!   (*The men have their backs to them and as she walks to door with* CICILY, *she says rapidly.*) My dear—I've something to tell you about a terrible old maniac—who is loose in this house—he thinks he's a cat!—Oh, I wish there was a train back to New York. (SUSAN *and* CICILY *exit.*)

CROSBY.   (*Continuing his conversation*)   Now I don't—think there is any danger, but it is just as well to be prepared —— (HARRY *starts to go.*) Where are you going, Harry?

HARRY.   (*At door*)   Out in the garden for a little air. (PAUL *goes, sits on sofa.*)

CROSBY.   (*Alarmed*)   But—suppose you run across this madman?

HARRY.   You mean the cat—if I do—I'll bark at him, and chase him up a tree! (*Grins at them in a peculiar manner.*)   I—I won't see you again, Mr. Crosby—I'm leaving early in the morning. Good-bye! (*Exits.*)

CROSBY.   Good-bye! (*To* CHARLIE.)   We had better go down and see that all the windows and doors are bolted ——

CHARLIE.   I'll be right along—I want to speak to Annabelle.

CROSBY.   Come on, Paul.

PAUL.   (*In reverie*)   Eh!

CROSBY.   Come on —— (*Exits.*)

PAUL. Well, I don't know that I'll be much use to you—but then again, I'm always nervous before going into action. (*Meets* ANNABELLE *at door.* CHARLIE *is looking out of window* L.)

ANNA. Paul, are you coming back?

PAUL. I hope so. (*Exits.*)

ANNA. (*Seeing* CHARLIE) Charlie, don't you want anything to eat?

CHARLIE. I'd rather talk to you while I have the chance. (*Closes door.*)

ANNA. (*Sits* R. *of table*) Go ahead!

CHARLIE. I don't know just how to begin!

ANNA. (*Smiles at him*) Then let's begin by asking you a few questions.

CHARLIE. (C.) All right!

ANNA. (*Looks at him intently*) What's the trouble between you and Harry?

CHARLIE. You.

ANNA. Oh, I thought it was something deeper than that—more important, you know.

CHARLIE. There's nothing in the world quite so important as you, Annabelle.

ANNA. That isn't so awfully good, Charlie.

CHARLIE. My dear, I'm not trying to flatter you. I was only speaking the truth. Our quarrel was about you. Of course I don't exactly blame him—he's jealous.

ANNA. Just jealousy doesn't explain this deadly hate that's sprung up between you and Harry—and I don't like it.

CHARLIE. The hate's all on his side—I've tried to make it up. But I'm afraid that's Harry's nature —he broods over the fact that I've cut him out.

ANNA. With me?

CHARLIE. Of course—I didn't tell him about it —he just sort of sensed it.

ANNA. Still you must have been quite sure that you had cut him out. (*Faces front.*)

CHARLIE. Why, I thought I had some reason to feel that—well—it *is* all right, isn't it? (*Crosses back of her and sits on table.*)

ANNA. It's all right to feel anything you choose, but isn't it taking a great deal for granted to think that I'm in love with you?

CHARLIE. Perhaps it is—but when you chased Harry off—and encouraged me ——

ANNA. And I don't mind owning up that for a while I was a *wee* bit foolish about you ——

CHARLIE. Thanks.

ANNA. And it might have got worse—you know, you have a way of making yourself rather attractive—and you did seem to be so fearfully sincere. Then—suddenly you changed. I couldn't make out what it was. You seemed worried about something. I thought it must be one of two things—another girl or money. But it couldn't be money—you're too successful.

CHARLIE. No, just successful enough—to get what I go after ——

ANNA. That's just it—what you go after. But you sort of let up going after me.

CHARLIE. You're mistaken, I never ——

ANNA. (*Rises and crosses to* C.) It was the other girl—(*Leaves envelope that* MAMMY *gave her on table. Turns.*) or girls—how many were there?

CHARLIE. None ——

ANNA. That's such an old one. Charlie! (*Crosses* R.)

CHARLIE. It doesn't make it any the less true ——

ANNA. All right—I'll take your word for that part—(*Sits on sofa.*) but the rest—I know—when it came—your growing coldness ——

CHARLIE. (*Going to her*) There was no such thing ——

ANNA. Then call it distraction—whatever you like ——

CHARLIE. But that passed and I came back—more in love with you than ever ——

ANNA. Yes, and I welcomed you—I tried to warm up the old affection. And only to-day I realized that it couldn't be done.

CHARLIE. You can't really mean ——? (ANNABELLE *looks and turns head away.*) Isn't there the slightest hope—ever?

ANNA. No! Fate has taken the matter out of my hands!

CHARLIE. You—you—really—love him?

ANNA. I can't help it, Charlie.

CHARLIE. Then I guess this is my finish. (*Moving* L.)

ANNA. Not unless you wish it.

CHARLIE. You think after this—we could be just friends?

ANNA. I wish you'd try.

CHARLIE. Very well, I'll try. Good-night, Annabelle.

ANNA. Good-night, Charlie. See you in the morning. (CHARLIE *exits.* ANNABELLE *puts out light* R., *crosses to table* L. *for envelope, sees book, opens book. Starts at what she sees.*) Fear! Eh! (*She reads, sits* R. *of table very much interested.* CROSBY *enters and starts up* R. *before he sees her.*) Paul. Oh, Mr. Crosby.

CROSBY. (*Pausing* R. C.) You here alone, Annabelle? I don't want to worry you, but there's something you ought to know.

ANNA. Won't it keep till morning, Mr. Crosby? (ANNABELLE *reading.*)

CROSBY. No—to-morrow may be too late. Annabelle! (ANNABELLE *looks at him.* ANNABELLE *smiles and continues to read.*) You know Mr. West was a very eccentric man—I have just made a discovery—it has convinced me it would be dangerous for you to be left here alone. (*Over to bookcase* R. *and feels along case for spring.*)

ANNA. (*Looking over her shoulder at him and laughing*) Mr. Crosby.

CROSBY. Don't laugh, Annabelle! (*Examining* R. U. *corner of bookcase.*) I know what I'm talking about, believe me. I'm alarmed—and I want you to take me seriously. (*Panel opens,* CROSBY'S *back is to it. He half turns toward* ANNABELLE.) Annabelle, you're in danger—great danger—but, thank God, I can tell you who they ——

(*Hand comes through panel and drags* CROSBY *off by throat.* CROSBY *disappears into panel which closes after him.*)

ANNA. (*Does not see what has happened but is interested in book. Finally, in vague sort of way, she becomes aware that* CROSBY *has stopped talking so she turns to answer him*) But, Mr. Crosby, I've heard so much about ghosts and spirits to-night that in spite of myself I'm growing nervous. And so that's why I'd rather not hear —— (ANNA-BELLE *looks up and finds herself alone. She is startled and rises.*) Mr. Crosby! Mr. Crosby! (*She goes to door and opens it.* MAMMY *is standing in door looking at* ANNABELLE *with a peculiar look.*) Where did Mr. Crosby go?

MAMMY. (*Enters and crosses* R. *of door*) I ain't seen him.

ANNA. (*Startled*) You haven't seen him? You must have passed him in the hall.

MAMMY. No, Miss West,. I passed no one in the hall, and I ain't seen Mr. Crosby. Are you sure he was in this room?

ANNA. (*Crosses* R. *of door. She is shaken*) Yes—yes—I was talking with him just a moment

ago. (*Goes to hall, calls.*)   Susan, Cicily, Paul!
Why do you look at me like this?

(CICILY *enters with* SUSAN. *She sees something
    has happened. She goes to* ANNABELLE.)

SUSAN.   What is it, Annabelle?
ANNA.   Was Mr. Crosby with you in the dining-
room?
CICILY.   No.   Only Charlie and Paul.   (PAUL
and CHARLIE *enter. Boys enter, cross to back of
table.* PAUL R.   CHARLIE L.)   Mr. Blythe is outside in the garden.   (*Looks at her keenly.*)   What's
wrong, Annabelle?
ANNA.   (*Trying to speak calmly*)   An extra-
ordinary thing has happened.   A few moments ago
I was sitting there, (*Points to chair R. of table.*)
and Mr. Crosby was there, (*Points up stage and
continues.*)   talking to me—when suddenly he—
vanished.   (*All look at each other.*)
CICILY.   (*Exchanges an alarmed look with
SUSAN*)   Vanished!   (SUSAN *sits chair R. of table.*)
CHARLIE.   (*Puzzled*)   Mr. Crosby vanished?

(PAUL *moves to back of* ANNA.)

ANNA.   Yes, he melted into the air.   I ran and
opened the door.   Mammy was standing there.
(*All look at* MAMMY.)   And she said that no one
had left the room.
MAMMY.   (*With a malicious look*)   I didn't see
anyone leave this room.
ANNA.   (*Wildly*)   But you must have heard him
talking to me when you came down the hall.
MAMMY.   I only heard you—talking to yourself.

(ANNABELLE *down* R.   MAMMY *exits, leaving door
    open.*)

SUSAN. (*Sitting* R. *of table.* *To* CICILY) **I'm** afraid Cyrus West wasn't the only lunatic in our family. (*Looks at* ANNABELLE.) When a woman begins to talk to herself, and to see people vanish right in front of her—it is curious.

CHARLIE. Are you trying to insinuate that Anna-belle is losing her mind?

SUSAN. (*Faintly*) Oh dear, oh dear.

ANNA. (*Crosses to* L. *of sofa*) You—you mean you don't believe me?

CHARLIE. (*To* CICILY) Certainly we do.

PAUL. Certainly.

ANNA. (*At sofa*) But you do think that I im-agined Mr. Crosby disappeared in front of me. If that's imagination—where is Mr. Crosby?

SUSAN. (*Crosses to* ANNABELLE) Probably out with Harry Blythe in the garden. My dear, you are upset and nervous—I didn't mean to say you were crazy—I was only trying to —— Come, Cicily, let us go to our room, and pile the furniture in front of the door. What with a dozen lunatics in the house, it will be a mercy if we're not all murdered in our beds. (*Exit with* CICILY.)

CHARLIE. (*Crosses to* ANNABELLE. PAUL *crosses up to panel, takes book and opens it as if to read*) Is there anything I can do?

ANNA. Yes—yes—please find Mr. Crosby!

CHARLIE. Where—was he standing—when he vanished?

ANNA. (*Points to the exact spot where* PAUL *is standing looking at them*) There. (PAUL *closes book with a slam and dashes madly round sofa* R. *and sits.*) Please try to find him.

CHARLIE. I'll do my best, Annabelle! (*Exits giving them a curious look, closes door.*)

ANNA. (*Crosses to front of table* L.) Paul You don't think I'm mad, do you?

PAUL. (*Rising—doubtfully*) Well, I guess I'd

get goldarned mad if some old chatter-box said I was crazy—but then again, if I really was crazy, I wouldn't have sense enough to get mad.

ANNA. (*Sighs*) You're such a help to me! Good-night!

PAUL. (*Crosses to* ANNABELLE) But I want to talk to you. I haven't had a chance.

ANNA. Your chance will come later—it's almost one o'clock.

PAUL. But I've got an idea ——

ANNA. Keep it until morning ——

PAUL. But it may not keep until morning.

ANNA. Run along now, and see if Mr. Crosby has returned. Good-night, Paul. (ANNABELLE *goes to chair at window.*)

PAUL. Annabelle, I really do think under the circumstances, honest to goodness —— Good-night! (*Goes up to door. Turns at door.*) I only wanted to say that now I am here and you're here, too, how awfully glad I was—glad I am—I mean that we both am—*was* —— Good-night —— (PAUL *exits.*)

(*As soon as* ANNABELLE *is alone, she goes to the bookcase where* CROSBY *was standing when he vanished. She looks along the rows of books, then she turns front, shrugs her shoulders and comes down* C. MAMMY *enters.*)

MAMMY. Mr. Crosby ain't come in yet.

ANNA. (*In front of chair* C.) Where can he be?

MAMMY. I know. It's got him—the demon in this house. *It's* here.

ANNA. (*Nervous*) Oh, don't—don't, please!

MAMMY. (*Crosses* R.) All right. Your room is ready and remember you've got to open that letter.

ANNA. (*Looks at letter*) Oh, yes! Unpack my bag, Mammy—I'll be right in.

(MAMMY *gives her a mysterious look, and goes out, closing door in.* ANNABELLE *crosses to table, looking at envelope, then* ANNABELLE, *sensing danger, reaches up and turns off the light, leaving herself in the dark with the maniac. She rushes to the door through the moonlight from the windows, opens it and dashes out, slamming the door. The monster's head appears above armchair* C. *as the*)

CURTAIN DROPS

ACT II

SCENE: *Bedroom next to library.*
TIME: *A few moments later.*
*A gloomy room with a four-poster bed up
stage, L. C. Fireplace L. Door R. C. Usual
tables and chairs.*
DISCOVERED: MAMMY *is taking* ANNABELLE'S
slippers out of suitcase on chair near window.
MAMMY *crosses to bed and puts slippers under
bed, muttering: " Rhonda! Rhonda! Spirit
of Evil! " Door opens and* ANNABELLE *enters
from library, holding book in her hand. She
shows a certain amount of apprehensive terror
—or fear. Something that frightened her—in
the other room. She closes door quickly and
then her fear leaves her as she sees the fire
and* MAMMY.

MAMMY. (*At bed—as she enters, looks inquiringly at* ANNABELLE) Why! What is it?

ANNA. (*Smiles and shakes her head*) It's
nothing —— (*Looks all around.*) Mammy, that
fire is an inspiration. You have no idea what a
difference it makes. (*Over* R.)

MAMMY. (*Fixing covers on bed—and looking at*
ANNABELLE *impassively*) It does make the room
more cheerful.

ANNA. (C. *Crosses to fireplace* L.) But wait
until I redecorate it—I'm going to have a real
boudoir here. Mammy, this is—the most wonderful
night of my life. I can't realize that I've inherited
this house and this estate and everything.

42

MAMMY. I hope you'll be happy here.

ANNA. (*Sees a large grandfather's clock in corner up* R.) What a darling old clock. (*Crosses* R. *to clock.*) Why, it isn't running!

MAMMY. That clock stopped—twenty years ago to-night—just as Mr. West died.

ANNA. (*Sets it with her wrist-watch and it starts ticking*) Let's see if it will go—I guess that's about right. Hear it—isn't that lovely? (*Listens to the tick-tock a minute.*) Hear it? It makes the room cozier than ever. (*Looks around.*) This house has character. (C.) Mammy ——

MAMMY. Yeh! (*Crossing to chair* R. C.)

ANNA. —and I'm beginning to love it—more and more every minute—(*Crosses* L. *and changes her tone.* MAMMY *works over to bag on chair* R. C.) in spite of—of—what the others said and in spite of what—just happened.

MAMMY. What was that?

ANNA. Nothing really—(*Over to* MAMMY R. C.) but—well, just a moment ago—when I turned off the light in the library—I felt—or rather sensed the approach of something—evil.

MAMMY. Evil?

ANNA. For a moment I felt trapped. (*Shudders.*) It was the same horrible feeling I had when I was a little girl—hurrying up the stairs in the dark—afraid something was going to catch me —— Mammy, do you think there could be anything in the house?

MAMMY. Yes, spirits! But there is two kinds. The good ones that help you and the others—like the one that was—behind you in the dark. That was the demon that's got into this house.

ANNA. Oh!

MAMMY. As long as you ain't afraid—it can't get you.

ANNA. (*Stoutly—crosses* L.) I'm not afraid—of anything. (MAMMY *business with suitcase.*)

MAMMY. (*With a sarcastic smile that only the audience sees. Finishes unpacking grip, closes it and puts it on floor of window* R.) Don't forget that letter—Miss.

ANNA. (*Takes it, with animation*) Oh, yes—(*Sits in armchair. Looks at it.*) Uncle Cyrus gave this to you twenty years ago!

MAMMY. (*Few steps* C. *In a peculiar voice, watching her narrowly*) Twenty years ago to-night—just before he died on that—bed!

ANNA. (*Rises. As she realizes she must sleep on that bed, she shivers and shows fear*) Oh!

MAMMY. (*Quickly. Few steps nearer* ANNA-BELLE) You is still a-scared ——

ANNA. No—I'm not—in the library just before you called, I picked up this book without knowing what it was—it seemed to open itself at this chapter—called " Fear."

MAMMY. Fear!

ANNA. Listen. (ANNABELLE *sits in armchair* L.) " Fear is a delusion—Fear, or the belief in fear can be controlled and eliminated by understanding."

MAMMY. You believe that? (*Coming* C.)

ANNA. (*Reads*) Yes, I do! " Only the ignorant suffer through fear." (*Skips a couple of pages and reads.*) " Take a bird—a canary in its cage—put it on a table—then let a cat jump up and walk around the cage, glaring at the canary. What happens? The canary, seeing its enemy so close to it, is frightened almost to death. But if it had understanding, it would know that the cat couldn't reach it while it had the protection of the cage. Not knowing this, it suffers a thousand deaths—through fear."

MAMMY. But you ain't in no cage.

ANNA. Yes, I am. I am surrounded and pro-

tected by my faith and philosophy and my friends.
I am not afraid.

MAMMY. But you *is* afraid for Mr. Crosby!

ANNA. (*Looks at* MAMMY *with a startled expression*) Why—why—I'd forgotten for a moment. Could he have—no—if he had—you would have seen him. (MAMMY *nods. With a note of entreaty in her voice,* ANNABELLE *continues.*) Are you—sure—you didn't see him go out? He must have gone—somewhere—but where? Mammy— (*Rises.*) I couldn't have imagined—that he was in the room with me, could I? (*Crosses c.*)

MAMMY. (MAMMY *shakes her head doubtfully*) No!

ANNA. He *was* there—(*Crosses* R. *of* MAMMY.) and—yet he's not in the house—but he couldn't have —— (*Desperately.*) Mammy, I tell you he was there!

MAMMY. I believe you, Miss.

ANNA. (*Looks at her sharply*) Well, if he *was* there—and you didn't see him go out—where is he?

MAMMY. I tell you—it—got him.

ANNA. (*Angrily—crosses* L.) Rubbish—how could a—spirit—if there was one there—take a man like Mr. Crosby—and—and—disappear with him? No spirit could do a thing like that.

MAMMY. How do you know it couldn't?

ANNA. Well—I just know—that's all ——

MAMMY. Huh! What was Mr. Crosby telling you—when he was taken away?

ANNA. (*Slowly—looking at* MAMMY *with frightened eyes*) He was telling me about—about some danger that was near me—oh!

MAMMY. (*With a sinister look of triumph*) You see! He was trying to warn you about—*it*— when *it*—got him.

ANNA. No—no. Impossible. (*Puts book and envelope on mantel.*) Absurd!

(*THREE SLOW KNOCKS AT DOOR. First knock,* ANNABELLE *wheels around, looking at door. Second knock,* MAMMY *looks at* ANNABELLE. MAMMY *looks front. Third knock,* MAMMY *looks at door and takes two steps toward door, when it opens and* HARRY *appears and speaks.*)

HARRY. Annabelle—may I come in?

ANNA. (HARRY *comes down* R. C. ANNABELLE *looking at* HARRY *keenly*) Yes! Yes! Where have you been?

HARRY. Out in the garden. What is this about Crosby ——

ANNA. He was talking to me in the library. I was sitting with my back to him so I couldn't see exactly what happened, but when he stopped talking—I looked around and he'd gone! Could—could—anything have taken him?

HARRY. Of course not. You don't believe in ghosts, do you, Annabelle?

ANNA. (*Uncertainly*) No—no! But I thought I'd ask you.

HARRY. (*Gives her a curious look*) As soon as I heard about it, I went to the library and looked around. There's no place he could hide—no closets or anything. I don't understand it. Are you sure he was in the room with you?

ANNA. Yes, of course I am. Why does everybody keep asking me that? (*Crosses* L. *to fireplace.*) It's all perfectly exasperating.

HARRY. Annabelle, you're just working yourself up needlessly. Crosby's an able-bodied man—he can take care of himself. Don't worry, it's all right.

ANNA. I hope so. What were you doing in the garden, Harry?

HARRY.   Just looking around.   Better lock your door to-night, Annabelle.

ANNA.   Why should I?

HARRY.   Just to be on the safe side.   Perhaps I had better sleep in the library.

ANNA.   (*Excitedly*)   Why should you?

HARRY.   Er—in case you needed me.

ANNA.   (*More excited*)   Why should I need you?

HARRY.   I don't know—you might get nervous, or something.

ANNA.   (*Almost hysterically*)   What about?

HARRY.   Oh, Lord, I don't know—well, anyway—(*Goes to door.*) if you want me—call.

ANNA.   Yes, I will.   What time do you leave in the morning?

HARRY.   Early.—May I say good-bye to you before I go?

ANNA.   (*At corner of bed*)   Yes, I wish you would.

HARRY.   (*Looks at her*)   Good-night, Annabelle.

ANNA.   Good-night.

HARRY.   Don't worry, it's all right.   (*Exits with look at* MAMMY *as he closes door.*)

ANNA.   (*To* MAMMY)   He wanted to tell me something—but he didn't dare.   I wonder what it was?   Heavens, everyone seems to be acting so strangely, I begin to think I must be losing my mind.   (*Cross to fireplace.*)

(MAMMY *looks fixedly at her without speaking.* MAMMY *is on her way to bed with* ANNA-BELLE'S *negligée when knock is heard; she puts negligée on bed and opens door.* SUSAN *and* CICILY *enter clad in their negligées.*)

SUSAN.   Oh, Annabelle!

ANNA.   (*Coming* C.)   Just a minute!   Mammy,

won't you please go and see if Mr. Crosby *has* returned—look in his room ——   (MAMMY *exits.*)
What is it—anything happened?

SUSAN. (*Taking* ANNA *to stool* L.) My dear—
I simply couldn't sleep. I just had to tell you—
that Charlie absolutely misunderstood me—he put
the wrong construction on a most innocent remark.
I never meant to say that you were really crazy—
I only thought that you were upset—my, my dear,
please say you understand!

ANNA. (*Kindly, but with double meaning—to
stool*) Yes—I understand—perfectly. (*Indicates
for them to sit down.*) Won't you sit down?

SUSAN. (*Sits in armchair.* ANNABELLE *sits on
stool.* CICILY *sits on chair near foot of bed*)
Annabelle—I feel it's my duty to tell you something ——

CICILY. (*Stops her—speaks quickly in low
voice*) Cousin Sue—you promised you wouldn't.

ANNA. (*Turns around*) What was that,
Cicily?

CICILY. (*Confused*) Why—why—nothing of
importance—Annabelle.

SUSAN. I feel it's my duty to ——

CICILY. (*Interrupts her. Rises*) Oh, your
duty!—It would be a lot better, Cousin Sue—if
once in a while you would think of other people's
feelings—instead of your duty. (*Goes* R C.)

SUSAN. Heavens! Hear the child rave. You'd
think I'd done something terrible. Cicily, where's
your respect for me?

CICILY. (*Tearfully*) I do respect you (*Coming
to* SUSAN.) but—but—I've felt so nervous ever
since I've been here—and you pick on me because
it's your duty—and, oh dear, no one understands
me! (*Sits chair at foot of bed.*)

ANNA. (*Pets her*) Come, come—Cicily—what's
it all about?

CICILY. Something—happened—that would make you nervous—if you knew ——-

ANNA. Anything serious?

CICILY. No—just something that was told me—about the ——

SUSAN. I am in duty bound to tell ——

CICILY. No, now, Susan ——

ANNA. And I don't want to hear it —— (*Rises.*) I don't want to hear it! If it will make me any more nervous than I am now. (*Over to window.*) I've had enough for to-night—Susan, you may tell me in the morning.

SUSAN. (*Asks abruptly*) Are you quite all right now—my dear?

ANNA. (*Looks at her puzzled*) Why, yes—of course—why do you ask?

SUSAN. I was anxious about you—you know you were—were a little—hysterical in there!

ANNA. (*Sees what she is driving at and smiles*) I'm all right, thank you.

SUSAN. Your health always been good—my dear?

ANNA. (*Brings chair down* R. C.) Splendid. I need good health to work the way I do—at my painting and dancing.

SUSAN. I suppose you've led a feverish life—down there in the village with those—those artistic folk?

ANNA. (*Smiles*) No—never had money enough for that. (*Sits.*)

SUSAN. Ever have black spots in front of your eyes?

ANNA. (*Smiles*) No ——

SUSAN. Ever feel dizzy? (ANNABELLE *shakes her head.*) Pains in the back of your head?

(ANNABELLE *looks at* CICILY.)

ANNA. No.

SUSAN. But you have terrible dreams—don't you?

ANNA. (*Laughs*) Only—when I sleep on my back.

SUSAN. Do you suffer much from hallucinations?—Come on, tell me!

ANNA. (*Seriously*) No—but I have—I don't know what you would call them—but they're ——

SUSAN. (*Eagerly*) Symptoms!

ANNA. (*Intensely*) That's it! I have them every morning—and every evening.

SUSAN. That's the dangerous time, my dear ——

CICILY. What are they?

ANNA. Every morning—as soon as I wake up—I have the queerest feeling, it's some feeling ——

SUSAN. (*Her eyes popping out in excitement*) Yes—you—I knew it—I knew it—where ——

ANNA. (*Points to her stomach*) Here—and the funny part of it is—it disappears—as soon as I've had my breakfast. (*Laughs and winks at* CICILY.) I was just fooling, Susan. I'm just an ordinary—healthy, normal girl. If I weren't so normal I'd probably be a better artist. Anything else you'd like to know?

SUSAN. I hope you're not offended at my questions, my dear? It's only because I take such an interest in you, *now that you're the heiress!* And I've been wondering if there really is anything in hereditary insanity. It's in our family, you know.

ANNA. (*Rises—laughing*) I'm afraid it's *missed our* side entirely, eh, Cicily? (*Placing chair near window.*)

CICILY. I don't know anything about that—but it certainly missed *our* side. (CICILY *looks at* SUSAN.)

SUSAN. Well—let us hope so —— Another thing, my dear—now that *you are* the heiress, men

will suddenly find that you are very attractive.
Beware of them, my dear—all of them.

ANNA. (*Laughing*) All of them?

SUSAN. All of them! Every man who tells you
he loves you—is only in love with your money—
they're all alike—there isn't a decent man in the
world.

CICILY. Oh, Cousin Sue—don't say that! There
are lots of nice men in the world. Who could be
nicer than those—three men?

SUSAN. (*Loftily*) Dumb-bells—my dear—all of
them—dumb-bells.

(ANNABELLE *goes to the window.*)

CICILY. (*Firing up*) I don't think so at all—I
think Charlie is awfully sweet.

SUSAN. An overgrown ribbon clerk—a bluff—
and as cold as a dead fish.

CICILY. You can't say that about Paul. (*Inter-est from* ANNABELLE.) He's real cute—and he has
such expressive feet.

SUSAN. Paul! He! He don't know anything—
not even his own mind. And he's as timid as a
rabbit, my dear. Never trust a man with wiggly
feet—they're treacherous.

ANNA. (*Laughing—goes* C.) Let's get them all
in. What about Harry?

SUSAN. He's the biggest fool of the lot. Every
time he looks at me he begins to laugh.

ANNA. (*With mock gravity*) Really? You
know men—don't you?

SUSAN. I do—and that's why I'm warning you
about these fourth- and fifth-rate cousins of yours.
(*Rises.   Crosses to* ANNABELLE.) Take my ad-
vice and get rid of them as soon as you can. Good-
night, dear—(CICILY *rises.*) and I hope you won't
have any more—more —— (*Goes to door, turns*

and, speaks firmly.)   Annabelle, I feel it's my duty
to tell you something ——

(CICILY *interrupts* SUSAN.)

CICILY.   Susan ——
SUSAN.   Don't you dare to interrupt me! Annabelle, they made me promise that I wouldn't tell
you about the dreadful maniac—who's prowling
around the house.

(ANNABELLE *aghast—the scene switches to the
serious.*)

ANNA.   What are you saying—a maniac—in this
house?
CICILY.   Yes—and the guard ——
SUSAN.   (*Comes to her*)   The guard from the
asylum was here, he had traced him to this house.
He's a terrible old person.   He thinks he's a cat—
and goes around ripping people wide open.   They
made me promise I wouldn't tell you but I felt it
my duty to warn you—because if we are all going
to be murdered in our beds—I think we ought to
know about it.
CICILY.   If there's anything in anticipation,
Cousin Sue—you've been murdered a dozen times.
ANNA.   So that's why Harry was so mysterious
—that's what he wanted to tell me ——
CICILY.   Harry wanted to warn us but Mr.
Crosby and Charlie wouldn't let him.
ANNA.   (*Almost to herself*)   I wonder if that
was what Mr. Crosby was trying to tell me
when ——
SUSAN.   (*With terror*)   Perhaps—perhaps—he
got Mr. Crosby ——
ANNA.   (*Gasps*)   Then he *must* be in the house.
SUSAN.   He must be.   (*Whispers.*)   He must

be sneaking around the hall—now—waiting to jump on us—I could scream ——

ANNA.   (*White but calm*)   Yes—if he got Mr. Crosby—then—he *must* be in the house.

SUSAN.   (*Hysterically*)   Maybe he's out there now—*waiting* for us.

(*DOOR BANGS and* PAUL *enters.   At bang a scream from the three girls as they fly over* L. SUSAN L. *corner,* CICILY L. *of* SUSAN *and* ANNABELLE *down extreme* L.)

PAUL.   (*Dashes in, slams door after him—white with terror and hair standing on end, he stammers in his fright.   Points at door*)   Out in the hall, out in the hall—something passed me—I couldn't see it—but I felt it, it touched me—I heard it breathe ——

SUSAN.   You did ——   (*Door knob rattles.*)

PAUL.   Look out.   (*All scream.*)

MAMMY.   (*Enters and fixes her eye on* PAUL) Why did you run away from me?

PAUL.   You!   Was it you—that passed me in the hall?

MAMMY.   Yes, sir!   (PAUL *falls in chair.* MAMMY *to others.*)   I was coming from Mr. Crosby's room—Mr. Paul saw me in the hall and he turned and ran like a mouse.

SUSAN.   (*With triumph*)   You were scared!

PAUL.   (*Rises*)   Well, I don't know that I was exactly scared—I may have been a trifle nervous— you see, I was just coming ——

MAMMY.   No, sir, you was going!

PAUL.   (*Few steps* R.)   Well—maybe I was ——

ANNA.   You see, Paul, you were frightened by an idea—a delusion.   You thought Mammy was a ghost and she frightened you.   Your fear was nothing but imagination.

SUSAN. (*Ex* ·*anges knowing look with* CICILY *and says soothingly*) Yes—yes, my dear, no doubt —you're right. But all the same if I were you I'd lock the door to-night and look under the bed. That's what I'm going to do.

ANNA. Really! (*Begins to laugh.*)

SUSAN. Don't laugh, my dear. I've never gone to sleep in my life without first looking under the bed.

PAUL. (*Going to her*) What do you expect to find there?

SUSAN. Why, a man, of course.

PAUL. (*Smiling*) Wouldn't that be terrible for the man?

SUSAN. Mr. Jones!

PAUL. And then on the other hand maybe it wouldn't. I don't know!

SUSAN. (*Glares at him, takes* CICILY's *arm and goes to door*) Come, Cicily, let us go to bed— we'll feel safer there. (*Exits.*)

CICILY. (*Wails*) I'm afraid to go up-stairs—in the dark.

ANNA. Mammy—go along with them—goodnight.

(CICILY *and* MAMMY *exit. Close door.*)

PAUL. (*Looks at* ANNABELLE, *suddenly embarrassed*) I wonder if—well, I guess it's all right, but on the other hand ——

ANNA. What's all right?

PAUL. My being here alone with you. (*Looks at her negligée and gulps.*)

ANNA. (*Crosses* L.) Of course it's all right. This isn't an ordinary occasion, and besides, we're cousins, aren't we? (*Sits in armchair* L.)

PAUL. Yes, we're fifth or sixth cousins. **But**

somehow you seem like a perfect stranger to me.
(*Crosses* L. *to* ANNABELLE.)

ANNA.   Is that why you acted so queerly when
we met in the other room?

PAUL.   Yes. It didn't seem possible that you—
were Annabelle West, my little—(ANNABELLE *looks
at him. Gulps.*) *the* little girl I used to know in
Wickford—so long ago.

ANNA. (*Looking front*)   It must have been all
of five years.

PAUL.   Five years and eleven months—(ANNA-
BELLE *looks at* PAUL.) yes, five years and eleven
months—since you left Wickford and went to New
York to study Art. Remember, you always wanted
to be a great artist or a trained nurse.

ANNA. (*Smiles and nods*)   And you were going to be a *great surgeon*—and so ——

PAUL.   I went to college and became a horse
doctor. The folks never did think I'd amount to
much—no—but on the other hand, well, I've got
ideas. I've got one now. (*Crosses to stool* L. *and
sits.*)

ANNA.   I'm sure you have! But—isn't—it
strange for us to meet like this—after five years?

PAUL.   Well, maybe it is strange—but I think it's
wonderful. I used to think about you a lot.

ANNA. (*Pleased*)   You did! Really! How
nice!

PAUL. (*Embarrassed*)   Yes—oh, yes—no doubt
of it—now that I remember—I did think of you—
often.

ANNA. (*Smiles*)   You don't seem to be quite
certain about it. Are you ever sure about anything?

PAUL. (*Seriously—swinging   stool   around*)
There's one thing—I'm dead sure about!

ANNA. (*Amazed*)   You mean that you're really
positive about something? (*Looking front.*)

PAUL. (*Intense*)   Yes, Annabelle—I—I ——
(ANNABELLE *looks at* PAUL. *Stops and gulps.*)
But on the other hand—you probably wouldn't be
lieve me.

ANNA. How do you know? You've never been
really serious with me. Why don't you try?

PAUL. (*Floundering*)   I am trying—but I don't
seem to get anywhere. I've been trying to ask you
something for the last five minutes.

ANNA. Then for Heaven's sake, stop rambling
around and ask me.

PAUL. I'm going to—just as soon as I get myself wound up.

ANNA. Paul—about how long does it take you
to wind yourself up?

PAUL. I don't know—exactly ——

ANNA. Evidently it's quite an operation ——

PAUL. Well—this time—it's taken me five years
—and eleven months and I don't know if I'm wound
up yet—but I'm getting set—to ——   (*Gulp.*)

ANNA. (*Exasperated*)   Paul—*what*—are you
trying to tell me?

PAUL. Listen—Annabelle—I ——   (*Gulps.*)
You know I'm only a vet. (ANNABELLE *nods.*)
But from doctoring horses and mules—I've learned
a great deal about women, I mean that all three
of them do a lot of things they shouldn't do and
without any reason.

ANNA. Yes.

PAUL. Yes.

ANNA. What *are* you trying to tell me?

PAUL. This—Annabelle ——   (*Gulps.*)   Did
Cousin Susie tell you about something that's going
on around the house to-night?

ANNA. You mean about spirits?

PAUL. (*Nervously*)   Well—not altogether
about spirits. You know, Annabelle, I'm not exactly afraid of spirits—but on the other hand you

can't see them—and —— (*Looks around as if expecting to see spirits.*)

ANNA. You mean about the crazy man?

PAUL. That's it. *I* couldn't tell you—but from my knowledge of women I guessed that Cousin Susie'd tell you because she had promised she wouldn't.

ANNA. Yes—she told me—and it hasn't cheered me up any. I wonder if he really is around the house, Paul?

PAUL. I—I don't know—I don't know—but what I want to tell you is that *I'll protect you.* I've handled wild horses and wilder mules and there isn't a spook or a maniac living that I'm afraid of —— (*GONG IS HEARD TOLLING THE HALF HOUR.* PAUL'S *knees are knocking together.* PAUL *rises and crosses* L.) Good Lord—that gong again.

ANNA. It's only the clock, Paul, see?

PAUL. (*Mops his brow, crosses* C.) Lord—I thought it was that other gong. The one Mammy said was tolling for someone's death to-night!

ANNA. (*Shudders*) Don't, Paul—please don't talk about it ——

PAUL. (*Crossing to her*) I'm awfully sorry ——

ANNA. (*Smiles*) You were saying that ——

PAUL. I was saying that I wasn't afraid —— (*Breaks off and grins at her.*) You know I'm lying, don't you? I'm scared stiff—but I'm always like that—I always get nervous when I go into action. Every time we went over the top I was paralyzed—but I had to go—scared or not. So scared or not—if that maniac is in your house, I'm going to get him.

ANNA. You always did fight for me, didn't you, Paul? Even away back there in Wickford when you used to carry my books to school!

PAUL. (*Sits on arm of chair*) I'll never forget those days.

ANNA. Remember the time big Jim Daly pulled my hair? (PAUL *nods.*) Remember how you flew at him? (*She doubles up her fists.*) And what a *terrible beating* ——

PAUL. *He* gave me. Yes—I'll never forget it. Seems I always got licked fighting for you. Well, I hope I have better luck (*A few steps* c.) with the lunatic—if I find him. Listen, Annabelle! If you hear a rumpus or anything, don't come out— just sit tight and yell like hell!

ANNA. I feel safe now, knowing *you* are protecting me. Good-night, Paul.

PAUL. (*Taking her hand*) Good-night.

ANNA. —And good luck if you find him.

PAUL. (*Up to door*) Thanks! I'll probably need it, if he finds me.

ANNA. Good-night, Paul.

PAUL. Good-bye!

ANNA. Good-bye? Won't I see you in the morning?

PAUL. God knows ——

(*Door opens, PAUL gives a startled "Ah!" and flies out the door. MAMMY enters and goes to dresser with glass of water.*)

ANNA. (*Seated in armchair*) There's a man, Mammy. He's just naturally frightened to death, but he conquers his fear!

(MAMMY *looks at her intently.*)

MAMMY. Don't forget that letter.

ANNA. Oh, yes! (*Starts for mantel. There's a knock—it stops her. KNOCK, MAMMY opens the door.*)

CHARLIE. (*Stands in doorway*) Did I interrupt you, Annabelle?

ANNA. Come in.

CHARLIE. You don't mind? (*Coming down L. C. MAMMY closes door and crosses to window.*)

ANNA. No, I'm glad you came. I wanted to see you. Charlie, what do you think has become of Mr. Crosby?

CHARLIE. I haven't any definite theory—I've been trying to figure it out. It's very puzzling—but I think he'll turn up all right. You are the one —I am worried about.

ANNA. That's very sweet of you—but why worry about me?

CHARLIE. Just the natural feeling a man has for the woman he —— (*Looks at her sincerely.*) Annabelle—you know how I feel—toward you. (*Reaches for her hand.*)

ANNA. (*Turns away*) Please, Charlie.

CHARLIE. This is a queer old house—and if— well, if you need me—just call. My room is at the end of the hall, you know.

ANNA. Thanks, Charlie, I know I can count on you. I guess I'll be safe with all the men guarding me. Harry just told me the same thing.

CHARLIE. (*Bitterly*) So he was here? Leave it to him to get anywhere first ——

ANNA. And, Charlie—I know all about that crazy man.

CHARLIE. So you know—about that ——?

ANNA. Yes.

CHARLIE. And—*he* told you ——?

ANNA. I'm not telling you who told me. (*Smiles.*) You ought to be able to guess.

CHARLIE. All right. Now—I'll be ready if you need me—because I'm not going to—I'm going to sleep with my shoes on. (*A few steps R.*) Anna-

belle—don't you think you could ever feel—a little
—a little —— (*Over to* ANNABELLE.)

ANNA. Please, Charlie—I'm very fond of you—
I'm awfully sorry.

CHARLIE. (*Looks at her sadly*)   Good-night—
Annabelle. (*Exits—closes door.*)

(ANNABELLE *goes up to bed and picks up negligée.*)

MAMMY. Don't forget that letter, Miss.

ANNA. Oh, yes —— (*Crosses to mantel—
takes letter from back of mantel.* ANNABELLE
starts to open letter. MAMMY *starts to go out.*)
Don't go—I want you to help me—just the negligée!
It's so late I'm not really going to bed—just lie
down. (*Opening envelope, reading.* MAMMY *gets
negligée from bed.*) "To my heir—man or woman
—as you read—pause and reflect that this is the
twentieth anniversary of the hour that my spirit
left my body ——" (*Looks up, impressed.*) "I
could take no earthly possessions with me—I was
compelled to leave them to you—my unknown heir
—your hour will come and you will follow me."
(ANNABELLE *becomes uneasy, gives a sickly laugh,
then continues reading.*) "In your brief span of
life, enjoy the glittering symbols of the world
which I have renounced." (*Looks up.*)   Oh—it
gives me the creeps. (*Looks at letter.*)   Here's a
verse. It's a little more cheerful. (*Reads verse.*)

> " Find the number beneath the vine;
> The sparkling gems forthwith are thine.
> Find the number; its rhyme is ' mine '! "

(*Looks up.*)   What a silly little verse; but it's the
key to the necklace—it must be. Come along,
Mammy—help me. (*Crosses to mantel, puts letter*

there.)   "Find the number beneath the vine?"
And then—what number rhymes with mine?

MAMMY.   Nine!

ANNA.   (*Thinking it over.   Crosses to* MAMMY
and unhooking dress as she goes)   Of course.
Nine rhymes with "mine." And the date—to-day
is the 27th—2 and 7—make 9—and—September—
is the—ninth month; nine *must* be the number.

MAMMY.   (*Putting negligée on her*)   But you
have two nines now ——

ANNA.   (*Crestfallen*)   True. (MAMMY *picks up
dress and folds it over her arm.*)   But two nines
make eighteen—and eight and one make nine. It
must be nine. Now I wonder where the vine is?
(*Business of looking around room. Sees where*
MAMMY *is looking.* MAMMY *looks at mantel.*)
There, Mammy?

MAMMY.   Nine!   (*Pointing to mantel.* ANNA-
BELLE *crosses to mantel.* MAMMY *puts dress on
chair at dresser and goes to door.*)   Need me any
more, Miss?

ANNA.   Not now, Mammy—if I want you I'll
call—beneath the vine —— (MAMMY *goes to door
and turns the knob and opens door. Nervously.*)
Oh, Mammy, put the key in this side of the door,
will you?

(MAMMY *changes the key from the outside of the
door to the inside, so* ANNABELLE *can look at
it.*)

MAMMY.   Good-night, Miss!

ANNA.   Good-night, Mammy! (*Crosses to door
and locks it, then goes to mantel and looks at scroll
work, thinking.*)   Beneath the vine—the vine—
the —— (ANNABELLE'S *eye notices on the carven
scroll work of the fireplace a vine. With growing
excitement she stands up and examines it, then she*

counts the little carven knobs from the edge of the mantel.) 1—2—3—4—5—6—7—8—9. (*The ninth is directly under the vine. She presses it, a secret recess opens, and reaching in, she pulls out a blazing necklace. She gazes at its beauty and stands in front of fire to examine it; she kneels and puts it round her neck. The door-knob is seen to turn slowly. She jumps to her feet, crosses to door, unlocks it—opens it quickly but there is no one there —she calls.*) Who's there? (*There is no answer but the echo of her own voice. The house is deathly quiet. Taken with a sudden terror she quickly closes door and locks it. She starts back to fire, gets her slippers from under the bed. She sits in front of fire and begins to put on slippers. When she gets first slipper on, there are heard three dull taps on door.* ANNABELLE *looks quickly at door but thinks it's her imagination. At second slipper, a scratching is heard on door.* ANNABELLE *rises, picks up book on mantel to reassure herself that there is nothing to fear. Then she starts to electric switch at* L. *of door but no one is there; she smiles and says:*) How silly. (*Then she kicks off slipper at lower end of bed, arranges the pillows. Then she puts out lights and gets into bed. After wriggling around for a moment to get comfortable, she takes off necklace and slips it under pillow—gives a sigh and relaxes into sleep. Then a long arm with a claw-like hand is thrust from the panel. With crooked fingers it reaches slowly, cautiously toward* ANNABELLE'S *throat as if to strangle her. As it touches her, she jumps up in bed. The arm disappears—the panel closes and she screams.*) Oh! Help! Help! (*She jumps from bed to the door. She tries to get out; when she finds she can't, she pounds on door in a frenzy, and calls.*) I can't get out—the key is gone! Paul, Charlie, Harry! Paul, Paul! (ANNABELLE *faints.*)

(*There is a slight pause then* HARRY *is heard running down the hall. He raps on the door saying:*)

HARRY.   Annabelle, Annabelle, did you cal'?
PAUL.   Harry, I heard Annabelle call.
SUSAN.   What is it, Annabelle?
CICILY.   What's happened?

(*All this time* HARRY *is pounding on door trying to open it.*)

CHARLIE.   Try the door, break it down!

(*Door is broken in and* HARRY, *with flashlight, followed by* PAUL, CHARLIE, SUSAN, *and* CICILY *dash in* HARRY *comes down* L. *of* ANNABELLE *with flashlight on her.* PAUL *to her.*)

PAUL.   (*Seeing* ANNABELLE)   Annabelle!
CHARLIE.   What is it?
PAUL.   She's fainted.   (PAUL *and* HARRY *lift her and* PAUL *places her in armchair* L.)
CHARLIE.   What's happened?
HARRY.   (*Turns on lights and looks at door*)   I don't know.   (*Flashing light on* MAMMY, *who is entering door.*)

(CICILY *crosses to* PAUL *with smelling salts, then she puts on* ANNABELLE'S *slippers.* SUSAN *down stage* R., *looking out of window.*)

CHARLIE.   (*Crosses and looks under side of bed*)   I heard her scream for help.
HARRY.   She's had a shock.
CHARLIE.   How did she get it?
HARRY.   (*Looking around stage* R.)   I don't

know. There's no one here! It couldn't be her imagination.

CHARLIE. (*Coming down* C. *Has been glaring at* HARRY *all this time, now speaks with a cold fury*) It must be her imagination.

HARRY. (*Turning to* CHARLIE. *Startled*) What do you mean ——

CHARLIE. That you told her ——

HARRY. Told her what ——

CHARLIE. Told her about the maniac after we'd all agreed to keep silent.

HARRY. (*Hotly*) I didn't ——

CHARLIE. (*Cuts him off*) Don't lie—you were here—you told her ——

HARRY. You're crazy. I didn't tell her a thing

CHARLIE. (*Violently*) You're a liar ——

(HARRY, *furious, starts for him with clenched fists.*)

CICILY. . (*Turning to them*) Charlie, you're wrong. Cousin Sue told her.

CHARLIE. (*Crossing to* SUSAN R. *Furiously to* SUSAN) So you're the one?

SUSAN. Yes, I'm the one. I told her because it was my duty, and I'd do it again.

CHARLIE. You ought to be gagged for the rest of your life. (*To* HARRY.) I was mistaken—I'm sorry ——

HARRY. (*With menace*) Save your breath— you'll need it later!

CHARLIE. (*Sneers*) Will I—really?

HARRY. Yes. You called me a liar. You'll have to make good for that.

PAUL. Sh! Quiet—Annabelle!

(*All stand and watch* ANNABELLE.)

CICILY. She's coming to ——

ANNA. (*Comes out of her faint, sobs and holds* PAUL *with a convulsive grip*) Oh! Oh!

PAUL. (*Soothes her*) There! There! Annabelle, what was it?

ANNA. (*Still dazed, looks wonderingly at them*) It came from the dark—it—it touched me. (*Points to throat.*) Here! (*Feels for necklace.*) It's gone!

SUSAN. What's gone—my dear?

ANNA. My necklace—the—the hand took it.

HARRY. What hand?

ANNA. (*Looks at him with frightened eyes and gasps*) I don't know—just—a hand.

SUSAN. (*With incredulity*) Just a hand! My dear Annabelle, you're raving again. It's nothing but your imagination.

CHARLIE. (*To* SUSAN) Sh!

ANNA. No—I saw it—it was here—it touched me ——

CICILY. (R. *of* ANNABELLE) But, Annabelle— if there was anything here—where is it now?

ANNA. (*Vaguely*) It *was* here—it—it took my necklace ——

CHARLIE. There was no one in here—when we broke in, Annabelle.

PAUL. If Annabelle says that something was here in the room—something was in the room! Now, the question is, what was it?

HARRY. (*Cynically*) Why not the maniac?

SUSAN. (R.) Ha! Even if he had been here— which he wasn't, what possible use would he have for a necklace? (*Few steps up stage.*)

CICILY. (*With pity—crosses to* SUSAN. PAUL *crosses to dresser for glass of water, gives some to* ANNABELLE *and puts it on mantel, then comes back to her*) Oh, the poor dear—isn't it a shame? What do you think, Charlie?

CHARLIE.   (*At window*)   I don't think she saw anything.

HARRY.   (*Crosses to* CICILY)   Well, I do. (*Doggedly.*)   She must have seen something—terrible to make her faint like that. Her imagination couldn't do it.

SUSAN.   (*Coming down between* CICILY *and* HARRY)   No!   But an unsound mind could! (*Looks at them in triumph.*)

CICILY.   (*Sadly*)   What!

SUSAN.   Ha—I've known all along that Annabelle was as crazy as a March hare.

(PAUL *looks at them.*)

CHARLIE.   That's absurd.

SUSAN.   It's true.   Didn't she say that Mr. Crosby vanished right in front of her?   (*Looks at them.*)   And now she says that a hand reached out and took her necklace.   Rubbish!   If anything was here—where did it go?   People don't disappear in the air—even if she says they do.   Annabelle is unbalanced.   (PAUL *looks.*)   And I for one am going to see that she is examined by a specialist!

HARRY.   You ought to be ashamed.

CICILY.   Oh, Cousin Sue!

SUSAN.   Don't Cousin Sue me!   All of you—every one of you—think just the same as I do—that Annabelle is crazy.   (PAUL *moves* C.)   Only none of you are honest enough to come right out with it.

(HARRY *goes up to dresser and puts flashlight on it.*)

ANNA.   (*Who has been listening to all this, suddenly stands up*)   So that's it—you all think I am mad.

PAUL.   I don't.

ANNA. I know you don't. (*Crosses to* C. PAUL *works over to* L. *of bed.* HARRY *and* CHARLIE *start to say something.* ANNABELLE *silences them with a gesture.*) You've had your say about me—now I'll have mine. I've been through enough to-night to drive anyone mad—and a few moments ago I was hysterical—but now I can think clearly. I'm going to tell you exactly what happened to me in this room and you're going to believe it. (*Pauses and looks at them. They all stand motionless, watching her.*) I found the necklace there— (*Points to fireplace.*) then—I felt something watching me. The door-knob turned when I opened the door—there was no one there—something was either trying to frighten me—or my nerves were getting jumpy. I looked under the bed,—nothing there—then I was certain it was my nerves. I turned out the light—and went to bed—and then— just as I was falling asleep—I felt an icy breath sweep over me—I opened my eyes and out of the darkness a long claw-like hand reached toward me —it came—nearer—and nearer—I was like a person in a dream—I couldn't move—it touched my throat—(*Her voice gradually gets higher in pitch. As she hits her climax.*) I jumped up—the hand disappeared with my necklace—I ran to the door— I couldn't open it—I screamed—and that's all I —— (SUSAN *gives* CICILY *a look and smiles.* ANNABELLE *sees this.*) You don't believe me—some of you think that--(*Glancing at* SUSAN.) I'm mad. I'm not—I'm as sane as anyone in this room. You must believe me—because what I've told you is the truth—so help me God. (*She waits a moment. No one speaks—but all look at each other with a certain amount of guilt. Then* ANNABELLE *resumes, with a new note in her voice—a note of triumph—a note of truth.*) And I'm going to prove it to you. The hand that took my necklace—

(*Turns and points toward bed.*) came out of that wall. (*Slowly she turns and goes to wall. Others watch her without moving. There is something about* ANNABELLE'S *personality that awes them to silence. She feels along the wall near the bed, her nervous fingers press here and there, trying to find the spring that will open the panel. After a moment's search she accidentally touches the spring, and as the panel starts to open, she steps aside with a cry of—*) There! (*Which is cut short by a gasp of horror as a dead body slowly falls forward into the room as the panel opens. All stand without moving, horror-struck at the discovery of the murder.*)

HARRY. (*Crosses to body, looks at the body's face and gasps in a low voice*) Crosby! Dead!

CURTAIN

ACT III

SCENE: *Same as* ACT I.

TIME: *A few moments later.*

DISCOVERED: MAMMY *opening door, allowing* PAUL *to enter, carrying* ANNABELLE, *who has fainted again. Then* MAMMY *goes down to table* L. *and turns on lamp.*

CICILY, CHARLES, SUSAN *and* HARRY *follow.*

HARRY *closes door.* CICILY *goes to table* R. *and turns on lamp.* CHARLIE, *at table* L., *pours out whiskey.* SUSAN *sits* R. *of table* L. HARRY *at door looking off* L.

PAUL. (*Puts* ANNABELLE *on couch and motions to* CHARLIE *on knees in front of sofa*) Give me that—over there.

(CICILY *offers him smelling salts. Points at bottle of whiskey on small table.* CHARLEY *comes over with glass of whiskey which* PAUL *refuses.* CICILY *takes glass and puts it on table* L. *All the others act in an abnormally quiet manner. They have just been through an abnormal scene* [CROSBY *murder*] *and they are trying to keep calm at the same time. They carry a terrifically tense atmosphere.* MAMMY, *alone, is impassive. She is like a sphinx.* HARRY *walks up and down the room;* CHARLIE *stands there—trying to think;* SUSAN *is almost out; she is sunk.*)

CICILY. (*Back of sofa*) Oh, isn't it terrible! Poor Mr. Crosby ——

69

(PAUL *takes salts from* CICILY.)

HARRY. (*Silences her with a gesture. At door.*
MAMMY *above table* L.) Yes—yes ——
    CHARLIE. (*Goes to* PAUL) Is she all right?
    PAUL. (*Shakes his head*) Hasn't come out of
it yet.
    CHARLIE. God!—what she has been through!
    CICILY. (*Wailing*) What are we going to do?
    HARRY. (C.) Wait a moment. (*Closes door.*)
I'm trying to figure it out. (*Goes up to* PAUL *and
looks at* ANNABELLE, *then turns to others.*) When
Annabelle recovers—no talk about—that—in there
—(*Points to other room.* MAMMY *moves to front
of small table* R. *of door.*) understand? (*All nod.*)
    PAUL. That's right—not a word to remind her
about it—she's been through enough to drive anyone *mad.* Harry, what do you think we ought to
do?
    HARRY. (*Speaking in a low tone*) Listen, all
of you—there's no doubt about our having company
in the house—Crosby's death proves that—and
Annabelle has been in terrible peril. But how did
he—or whatever it was—get in there? (*Looking
at* MAMMY.)
    PAUL. God knows. Crosby and I locked every
window and door. Then after you started for bed,
I went through the house but didn't see or hear a
thing.
    CHARLIE. (L. *of sofa*) Of course you didn't.
The maniac—or whatever killed Crosby—was hid-
ing behind that panel.
    HARRY. That's just what I'm coming to—that
panel. I'm wondering if it would be best to explore
it now—or to wait for the police? (*Opens door.*)
    CICILY. Don't go in there and leave us alone.
    HARRY. There's probably no one in it—now—
and yet—there may be something we don't ever

dream of —— (*Opens door and looks across hall.*)

SUSAN. (*Wails*)   Close the door.

(HARRY *closes the door, stands* R. *of it, looking off* L.)

PAUL.   I know what I'm going to do just as soon as Annabelle recovers.

CICILY.   Oh, is she all right?

PAUL.   Well, she's breathing regularly—and her color's coming back.

CHARLIE.   What *are* you going to do?

PAUL.   I'm going through that panel, and I'm not going to wait for anybody—not even the police.

HARRY. (*Slams door and comes down* C.)   Just a moment—now think it over, according to the law—no one is supposed to enter a room where a murder has been committed until the police arrive. You probably wouldn't find anything there—anyhow—and you might disturb some valuable clues.

CHARLIE. (*Turns to* HARRY)   For once I agree with you; whoever killed Crosby probably beat it. It isn't natural to believe that the murderer would wait behind that panel to be caught.

HARRY.   Even if we found him there—we'd probably have to kill him ——

SUSAN.   Oh!

HARRY. (*Continuing*)   —defending ourselves, Miss Sillsby.   No, we'd better wait. (*Opens door and looks off* L.)

SUSAN. (*Moaning to herself*)   Oh, oh, what a terrible night.

CHARLIE. (PAUL *crosses* R. *to back of sofa, and* CICILY *comes round to front of sofa, sitting* L. *of* ANNABELLE.   *Crosses to* SUSAN—*sternly to* SUSAN)   Miss Sillsby—look at me!   Look at me!

Are you now convinced that Annabelle really saw everything she said she did? Answer me.

SUSAN. Yes—yes ——

CHARLIE. Then don't you ever open your mouth again about her being unbalanced—do you hear me?

SUSAN. Yes—yes ——

CHARLIE. Now the first thing to do is to get the police and a doctor —— (*Goes to telephone back of table.*)

SUSAN. (*Rises*) The police! And I'm in a negligée!

HARRY. (*Opening door wide and standing L. of it*) Well, you have plenty of time to change.

SUSAN. (*Up to door*) Yes, of course!

CICILY. (*Rises and takes a few steps toward door*) But I'm afraid to go upstairs.

MAMMY. I'll go with you, Miss.

SUSAN. Come on, Cicily. Let's pack up and get out of this terrible house. (SUSAN *exits.*)

CICILY. Mammy, you go first.

(MAMMY *and* CICILY *exit.* HARRY *closes door a little, looking off* L.)

CHARLIE. Are we all agreed that it's better to keep out of there—until they come? (HARRY *nods.* CHARLIE *takes 'phone.*) Hello! Hello! Must be out of order.

HARRY. Probably cut.

CHARLIE. It's all right now.

HARRY. Outside. (*Closes door.*) Paul! (*Comes down* C.) Did you and Crosby fasten all the cellar doors when you were downstairs?

PAUL. There was only one door. It has a bolt on the inside and I bolted it.

(*Suddenly a noise is heard downstairs like the banging of a shutter in the wind—all listen. Two slams of door.*)

HARRY. (*Cautions silence and they listen*)
Hear? That! (*Door slams again—one slam.*)

PAUL. Sounds like a door swinging against the
house in the wind.

HARRY. Listen! I think our—guest—has left
us—without closing the door. You locked the door,
Paul—it couldn't have opened unless *he* went out.
He probably escaped while we were talking here.
I'm going to see. (*Starts for door.* PAUL *goes
back of sofa to* ANNABELLE.)

CHARLIE. I'll go with you.

HARRY. No, you stay here and watch that door
—in case—I'm mistaken.

CHARLIE. But—I want ——

HARRY. (*Insolently*) Do as you're told.

CHARLIE. (*Furiously*) Why should I take orders from you?

HARRY. Because I'm giving them to you.

CHARLIE. (*Begins to smile*) Oh, I see. Now
that you believe it's safe—you're going to be a hero
in front of Annabelle ——

HARRY. (*White with anger*) Go down and do
it yourself.

CHARLIE. (*Taunting him*) Oh, I couldn't rob
you of that—honor.

HARRY. Just—just come along with me—will
you—I want to—talk with you—alone.

CHARLIE. Yes, and I want to ——

PAUL. (*Rushes over between them*) Here, cut
it out! Maybe I'd better give the orders from now
on—you fellows don't seem to be able to do anything—except snarl at each other. I'm not much of
a hero—but at that—I reckon I'm as good as either
of you. You fellows look after Annabelle. I'll go
and see about that door.

(*Two men watch him as he exits.*)

ANNA. (*Coming out of a faint*) Oh! Oh!
HARRY. (*Crosses to back of sofa*) Annabelle!
CHARLIE. Annabelle! (*Crosses to L. of sofa.*)
ANNA. (*Opens her eyes and looks at them. She smiles bravely at them*) Where's Paul?

(HARRY *back of sofa* R. CHARLIE *down* L. *of sofa.*)

HARRY. (*Fixing cushions*) He'll be back in a moment.
CHARLIE. Are you all right, Annabelle?
ANNA. (*Calm*) I feel very weak. Did I faint again?

(MAMMY *opens door slowly as though she were listening, then stands in door.*)

CHARLIE. (*Nods*) Yes. Just after Mr. Cr——
HARRY. (*Silences him*) Sh——!
ANNA. Is he—still there——
HARRY. (*Nods*) Yes—and no one must go in there until the police come.
ANNA. Did you telephone for them?
CHARLIE. The wires have been cut.
ANNA. The wires are cut?
CHARLIE. Yes—but I'm going after the police myself—soon as Paul comes back.
HARRY. I think the most important thing to do is to get a doctor. (*Looks at* MAMMY.) Mammy, can you tell me where the nearest doctor lives?

(CHARLIE, *in front of sofa, helps* ANNABELLE *to sitting posture. Very attentive to her.*)

MAMMY. I could tell you—but you'd never find it—I'll go if Miss West wants me to. (*Starts to go.*)

HARRY. But, Mammy, aren't you *afraid?*

MAMMY. (*With a peculiar smile*) Afraid! Me what's lived alone in this house for twenty years! (*Starts to exit.*)

CHARLIE. (*Stops her*) Wait a minute, I'll go with you. (HARRY *stands behind chair* C. CHARLIE *up to* R. *of door*.) Is the doctor's house near the police station?

MAMMY. (*To* L. *of door*) No—you go to the village—I go the other way. If you'll come with me—I'll show you the road.

(PAUL *enters, goes to* ANNABELLE. CHARLIE *down* C.)

PAUL. (*Down to* ANNABELLE) Are you all right, Annabelle?

ANNA. Yes. Mammy is just going for a doctor ——

HARRY. (*Coming down* C.) Paul! What did you find?

PAUL. (*Few steps over to* HARRY) You were right. The door was open. It must have been opened from this side, because I'm positive I bolted it myself when I was down there. Mr. ——

HARRY. Sh!

PAUL. Never mind.

ANNA. What is it?

PAUL. (*Explains to* ANNABELLE) We heard a door swinging against the house. The one I locked to-night. I went down and found it open—so I locked it again, that's all.

HARRY. (*Crosses to back of table* L.) I don't think there's any doubt now but that our guest— has left us—I think we are all pretty safe now—eh, Paul?

PAUL. (*Doubtfully*) Well, maybe we are—but then on the other hand—you never can tell.

ANNA. (*Shudders*) I'll never feel right again —until Mr. Crosby —— (*Looks toward the other room.* PAUL *sits* L. *of* ANNABELLE, *comforting her.*)

CHARLIE. The police will attend to all that, Annabelle. I'll be back as soon as possible. Come, Mammy. (*Up to door.* HARRY *above table.* MAMMY *exits.* PAUL *takes* ANNABELLE'S *hand.* CHARLIE *speaks to* HARRY *in a low voice.*) I don't want any more words with you than I can help— but while I'm gone—you just look after Annabelle.

HARRY. (*Smiles*) There's no more danger ——

CHARLIE. How do you know? The maniac may be in the house now. The open door doesn't prove that he's gone ——

HARRY. (*Loses his smile and he looks at* CHAR-LIE) You're right—he may still be here.

CHARLIE. And do you realize that another shock like she just had—might kill her—*or drive her insane?*

HARRY. (*Nods*) Yes—another shock might kill her or she might be ——

CHARLIE. Yes, she might—or *someone else might.* Until the police get here—look out for that room and don't believe yourself too safe. (*Starts for door.*)

HARRY. I know—you don't have to tell me. (*Looking front.*)

CHARLIE. (*Coming down to* HARRY. *Angrily but keeping his voice down*) I'm not telling you— because I'm worried about *you.* (*Exits.*)

ANNA. (*To* HARRY) Has Susan gone?

HARRY. (*Coming down* L. *to front of table*) No, but she's threatening to go. I believe she's packing up.

ANNA. Oh, I hope she goes—(*Rises.*) you can't imagine how nervous she makes me.

PAUL. (*Rising*) Oh, yes, I can—she makes me nervous. *I can't make her stop* talking.

HARRY.   Suppose she won't go? It's still dark.
ANNA.   (*Crosses to* HARRY) You must make her go.
HARRY.   What!
ANNA.   I'll feel so much better when she's out of the house—Paul!
PAUL.   (*Suddenly*) Harry, I've got an idea. If she stalls about being afraid to go to the station before daylight—*you* take her.
ANNA.   (*With animation*) Splendid—that gives her no excuse for not going.
HARRY.   Great Scott!! Have you people got a grudge against me?
ANNA.   You'll do it for me, won't you?
HARRY.   (*Sighs*) Yes, if you really want me to —— (*Looks at her keenly.*) Sure you won't be nervous—staying here alone?
ANNA.   Alone! You forget—I have Paul.
HARRY.   (*Looks at* PAUL *with a curious expression, and replies in a peculiar voice*) Oh, yes ——
SUSAN.   (*Enters, dressed for the street, followed by* CICILY. *To* ANNABELLE. *At door*) Have the police come? (ANNABELLE *crosses* R. *in front of sofa*—PAUL L. *end of sofa.* HARRY *moves* L. *to back of table.*) Oh dear! What a night! (*Coming down* R. C. *There is silence for a moment, then she starts again.*) I just know it—I felt it in my bones—the minute I entered this terrible house that something would happen. And just to think it had to be poor Mr. Crosby—(*Turns* L.) and it might just as well have been—(*Looks at* HARRY.) you! (PAUL, *growing uncomfortable, tries to stop her talking by glaring at her.* HARRY *stands listening with a cynical smile.* CICILY *nervous.* ANNABELLE *very nervous.* CICILY *up stage* C.) It's a wonder we weren't *all* murdered.
CICILY.   Poor Mr. Crosby!
SUSAN.   And I'll never forget to my dying **day**—

how he pitched out of that panel—nearly into your arms, Annabelle!

(ANNABELLE *gives a nervous start.*)

PAUL. (*Firmly*) Miss Sillsby—stop talking.

SUSAN. (*Flaring up*) Mr. Jones—to whom are you speaking?

PAUL. To you. I'm the boss around here and I command you to—to—to dry up. (*To back of sofa.*)

SUSAN. (*Glares at both of them*) Well, I never! In all my born days I never —— (*She is speechless for a moment, then turns to* CICILY.) Come, Cicily—now, we're packed up, let's get out of this terrible house. (*Few steps toward door—then turns down to* ANNABELLE.) I'm so sorry to leave you, dear ——

ANNA. (*Smiles at her*) That's nice of you--but I'll be all right.

SUSAN. Perhaps I had better stay here after all.

(HARRY *and* PAUL *exchange looks of dismay.*)

ANNA. Don't stay on my account. The doctor will be here soon ——

SUSAN. But I wonder if there'll be any trains—it isn't dawn yet.

HARRY. (*Back of table at* R. *end of it. Smoothly*) If you hurry you've got just about time to catch the milk train ——

SUSAN. Milk—train! I never rode on a milk train in my life!

PAUL. You ought to try anything once!

CICILY. But I'm afraid to go and now—it's still dark.

HARRY. Miss Sillsby—if you're really anxious to go—I'll be only too happy to see you and Miss Young to the station!

CICILY. Oh! Will you—really? (*Crosses to* HARRY *and takes his arm.*)

SUSAN. (*Scornfully*) Young man—I'll allow you to come with us on one condition. You may talk with Cicily if she will let you—but—I'll have nothing to say to you.

HARRY. (*Huskily*) Can I depend on that?

(SUSAN, *with a sniff, turns away.* CICILY *goes up to* R. *of door and* HARRY *to* L.)

SUSAN. (*Marches to* ANNABELLE) Well, Annabelle—I am glad you are all right because I was afraid the next time I saw you—you'd be non compos mentis. Good-bye, my dear. I hope you'll soon be well again—but I'm afraid you won't —— (SUSAN *exits.*)

CICILY. Good-bye, Annabelle! (CICILY *exits, followed by* HARRY, *who closes door.*)

PAUL. (L. *of sofa at back*) She's just a nice little pal!

ANNA. I don't think she's half—as—as malicious as she seems to be, do you?

PAUL. Well, I don't know. *Maybe* she's only one-half—but—on the other hand, I think she's one hundred per cent. poison.

(*Pause while they look at each other and gradually realize they are quite alone in the house.*)

ANNA. It's rather nice to be alone—isn't it, Paul?

PAUL. Yes, sir, it certainly is—(*Shivers.*) but it's kinda quiet, though ——

ANNA. This is the first time we've been really alone to-night.

PAUL. (*Smiles*) It's the first time—we've been really alone since you left Wickford.

ANNA. What was it you—wanted to tell me?

PAUL. When?

ANNA. To-night—don't you remember, you said you had an idea.

PAUL. (*Crosses his brows trying to remember*) That's right—I did have an idea then—but it's gone now.

ANNA. That's nothing—you'll get another.

PAUL. I'm not so sure about that—ideas are scarce with me.

ANNA. (*Smiles*) Really.

PAUL. (*Soberly*) Yes. Up at college—they used to say I only got one idea a week but let me tell you right now when I *do* get one—it's a bear.

ANNA. What was this last idea about? (*Moving over to R. of sofa and indicates for PAUL to sit down.*)

PAUL. It was about you —— (*Sits beside her on sofa.*)

ANNA. Me! (*Looking at PAUL. PAUL moves away from her.*)

PAUL. Yes—now wait a minute. (*Thinks a moment, then the silence gets oppressive. Whistles.*) Gosh! It's quiet in here—I never knew a house could get so quiet. (*Looks all around, and as he looks at door, he gives a nervous start, and quickly looks at ANNABELLE, who is watching him.*)

ANNA. (*Seems as if she were listening for something—speaks in a low tone*) Was that—that door really open—downstairs?

PAUL. Yes—and I closed it and bolted it. (*Chokes a little. Rises, back a few steps.*) You didn't—want me to—to—go down and see again?

ANNA. No—no —— (*Pause.*)

PAUL. (*Looks at whiskey*) Thanks—I mean much obliged. I think I need a drink. Do you mind —— (*Crosses to back of table. ANNABELLE shakes her head—still listening. Fills glass and drinks half.* PAUL *coughs and chokes—but it has an almost immediate effect on him—as shown in his bearing and in the tone of his voice.*)

ANNA. (*Crosses to chair* R. *of table* L.) Paul, do you really think that—it—is out of the house?

PAUL. Now, Annabelle—you mustn't think about it.

ANNA. Tell me, Paul—are we—are we safe?

PAUL. (*With confidence*) Of course—now doesn't it stand to reason that—the door couldn't open itself? Of course it's gone—don't think about it.

ANNA. But suppose it *didn't* go out. (*Sits in great excitement.*)

PAUL. Annabelle, you're getting nervous. (PAUL *drinks half of what's left in glass. Business of putting stopper in decanter—then the stimulating effect to drink.*) You know it's wonderful—wonderful how all my ideas are coming back to me. (*Stopple business.* PAUL *thinks a moment, then snaps his fingers.*) I've got one ——

ANNA. Tell me.

PAUL. (*Leans forward in his excitement. Looking front*) The *whole thing just struck me as being darned queer.*

ANNA. What?

PAUL. Everything. Right straight through from the start to finish.

ANNA. You mean ——

PAUL. From the time the will was read to-night —until now ——

ANNA. (*Interested*) Yes.

PAUL. Remember when you were declared the heiress? (*Seated on back of table, facing* ANNABELLE.)

ANNA. Yes.

PAUL. Remember the codicil? (ANNABELLE *nods.*) That if anything happened to you—or you

were to lose your mind or anything—the estate was
to go to the next heir?

ANNA. Yes, yes, I remember ——

PAUL. And his or her name was in the third
envelope ——

ANNA. You mean the one that Mr. Crosby put
in his pocket when he said, " I trust that this shall
never be opened!"

PAUL. Exactly. And from that moment on,
things began to happen to you ——

ANNA. And to Mr. Crosby ——

PAUL. (*Sitting on edge of table*) Because he
was the one who drew up the will—and he was the
only one—who *knew* the name of the next heir—unless—(*Rises.*) *maybe* (*Crosses* R. C.) and then again
maybe not.

ANNA. (*Turning in chair to face* PAUL) Paul
Jones—what are you saying?

PAUL. (*Silences her with a wave of his hand*)
Didn't I tell you that while my ideas are scarce—
when I do get one it's a humdinger?

ANNA. Heavens—you don't mean ——

PAUL. I'm liable to mean anything. Listen.
This is just an idea of mine, but you never can tell
—it may lead us somewhere. All right! Things
began to happen to you in this house to-night, what
for? To scare you.

ANNA. You mean someone was —— Oh!

PAUL. Just a minute. Crosby got on to this
plot—he tried to tell you—before he finished, something happened to him—then gradually all of them
—I don't say they did it intentionally—but they
started to think and to say that you—were unbalanced.

ANNA. And you mean—that all this was a plot
to frighten me ——

PAUL. I don't know—I don't know. (*Goes* R.)

I'm just trying to figure it out. Just seeing where my idea will carry me.

ANNA. Yes, yes, go on.

PAUL. Now, just suppose that someone—call it the next heir—-thinks that you—might possibly have inherited—the family ——

ANNA. You mean—the family failing.

PAUL. Exactly—and they—that is he—she—it—well, someone starts to frighten you—hoping to shock you into—or worse—then—it discovers that Crosby is on the plot—so it—kills Crosby.

ANNA. (*Rises*) No! No! Impossible!

PAUL. Why is it impossible? The door-knob turning—locking you in your room—the panel—the hand —— (ANNABELLE *gives a little cry of terror.*) I'm awfully sorry, but don't you see—it *is* possible? The whole thing might have been arranged to frighten you into ——

ANNA. No, no. How can you explain about that bell—and Mammy's warning of Mr. Crosby's death?

PAUL. They might have all been planted. (*Crosses to* R. C. *Thinking.*) They might have all been planted—they -—— (*Pause.*) Give Mammy Pleasant a thought.

ANNA. Mammy Pleasant! Why, she's not the next heir?

PAUL. How do you know she's not? She might be—besides your necklace alone is worth a fortune. She might be the next heir.

ANNA. (*Silent a moment, thinking. A few steps to* PAUL) But—that old man who had escaped from the asylum—how did ——

PAUL. He might have been brought here to frighten you—*now suppose—just suppose that*— (ANNABELLE *gives a little cry.*) now don't get nervous—but just suppose that Crosby had brought him in the house ——

ANNA. (*Stops him. Crosses* R. *in front of* PAUL *to front of sofa*) No—no—don't, Paul ——

PAUL. (*Turning to her*) Now don't get so excited, I'm just supposing, that's all. Suppose Crosby had brought him into the house, then the maniac suddenly grew violent—turned on Crosby—and *killed him* ——

ANNA. Oh, no!

PAUL. (*Long pause. Crosses to chair* R. *of table* L.) *On the other hand*—suppose *I* were the next heir ——

ANNA. (*Smiles at him. Sits on sofa* L.) Now, I *know* you're joking.

PAUL. (*Crosses to table* L.) Well—I can tell you right now it's not me—now who's left—(*Sitting at table* L.) Susan! Charlie! Cicily! Harry! Take your choice.

ANNA. It's fantastic—absurd.

PAUL. Well—maybe it is—but then again maybe it isn't. But there's one thing I'm dead sure of. Your brain is one hundred per cent normal. If there's any insanity in this family—it's not in you. But the more I think of it —— (*Thinks a moment, then snaps his fingers.*) I've got another idea. (ANNABELLE, *in alarm, leans forward.* PAUL *crosses to sofa.*) But I'm not going to tell you about this until I'm sure of it. But—part of my idea is this—*law or no law,* I'm going in there—and get that envelope out of Crosby's pocket and find out who *is* the next heir. (*Starts for door.*)

ANNA. (*Rises and holds* PAUL) No—no—don't leave me.

PAUL. (*Brings her to couch*) I won't be gone a minute. I'll leave both doors open and nothing can possibly happen—but, mind you, nobody must know that I've been in there, especially the police—understand? Now don't tell a soul. I'll be right back! (*As he opens door.*) See, I'll leave both doors open; I'll be right back.

(*Sees him cross th 2 hall and go into the other room. ANNABELLE sitting on sofa. Waits for him, looking at door, then she turns her head away a moment. As ANNABELLE turns her eyes from the door—A TALL MAN [DOCTOR PATTERSON] in black clothes, wearing a black hat, glides into the room without making any noise and stands looking at her. ANNABELLE turns and sees this man—she shrinks in terror.*)

PATTERSON. (*Coming down* c.) Miss Annabelle West?

ANNA. (*Whispers*) Who are you?

PATTERSON. I'm Doctor Patterson—your maid just brought me over. (*Putting hat on chair* c. *Comes over and looks at her with a professional eye.*) She told me you were here—so I walked in —did I frighten you?

ANNA. (*Trying to conceal her fears for* PAUL) Yes—no—I thought it was ——

PATTERSON. I see—your condition is more serious than I thought. (*Looks in her eyes a moment.*) You've been under a nervous strain! (*ANNABELLE stares at him, petrified by fear.*) Humm! (*Takes a small pocket flash and holds it near her eyes. Flashes it in her eye and watches the pupil dilate and recede.*) H'mm!—Your eyes hurt you. (*Takes her pulse.*) Very quick action. (*MAMMY enters with glass of water.*) Were you excited?

ANNA. (*Shakes her head*) No.

MAMMY. Feeling better, Miss West?

ANNA. (*Relieved at sight of* MAMMY) Yes— yes ——

PATTERSON. I'll take that. (*Crosses to* MAMMY *and takes glass. Indicates with nod to* MAMMY *to get out.* MAMMY *exits, closing door.*) H'mmm! Very strange. (*Crosses back of sofa, puts glass on small table* R. *Works down round table* R. *to front of sofa.*)

ANNA. Strange?

PATTERSON. Yes—your actions—your eyes suggested a terrible worry—or anticipation—you act as if you recently had a shock. (*Putting pill in water.*)

ANNA. Didn't—Mammy tell you about me—about the—the ——

PATTERSON. Miss West, I never discuss my patients with their servants. Besides, your maid told me nothing. I think she's dumb. As I was saying, your physical condition is normal—but your mental —— Tell me about yourself.

ANNA. (*Hysterically—crosses* C. *to front of chair* R. *of table*) Oh, I can't stand it any longer. Why doesn't he come out? He went there. (*Points.*)

PATTERSON. (*Watching her keenly—crosses to* ANNABELLE) He? Who?—and where—is—there ——?

ANNA. Paul—went in there—that room where—where—Mr. Crosby was murdered. Charlie went for the police. Don't tell them.

PATTERSON. (*Observing her narrowly*) I won't—murder—police—yes—he is in there—with the dead body—what for?

ANNA. To get the envelope ——

PATTERSON. Yes—the letter ——

ANNA. No—the will ——

PATTERSON. All right—and you're afraid ——? Of something in that room?

ANNA. (*Down* L.) Don't ask me any more questions. Go—Paul! (PATTERSON *gives her another look and goes toward the other room.* ANNA-

BELLE *waits; as* PATTERSON *reaches door, he turns and looks at* ANNABELLE.)   Hurry!

(PATTERSON *exits.*)

PATTERSON.   (*Returns, carrying unconscious body of* PAUL)   He was lying on the floor. (ANNABELLE *helps put* PAUL *on couch.   Examines* PAUL's *head.*)   Nasty bruise.   (*Gets out bandages.*)   He must have tripped, and as he fell, he probably struck his head on the corner of the table. (*Bandage business.*)

ANNA.   (*Back of sofa.   Cannot restrain herself any longer*)   Was he lying near—near ——

PATTERSON.   Near what?   (*Cutting bandage but not looking at her.*)

ANNA.   The—body ——

PATTERSON.   What body?

ANNA.   (*Shrilly*)   Mr. Crosby—he was murdered there to-night.

PATTERSON.   Drink this—it's merely a sedative. (ANNABELLE *obeys him.*   ANNABELLE *sits* L. *of* PAUL.)   Miss West—your nerves are completely upset.   There was no one in that room but this young man.   (*Sticks adhesive tape on* PAUL's *forehead.   Smells* PAUL's *breath.*)   Did you have some? (*To* ANNABELLE.   ANNABELLE *shakes head.*   PATTERSON *grins.*)   The young man probably had too much.   He'll come round in a minute.

(PAUL, *after a moment, opens his eyes, looks blankly at them and asks.*)

PAUL.   What time did the eclipse take place?

PATTERSON.   How do you feel now?

PAUL.   Did you hit me?

PATTERSON.   No—you must have hurt yourself on the table.

PAUL. Nothing of the kind! Nothing of the kind! (*To* ANNABELLE.) Somebody hit me from behind when I went in to get that envelope from Crosby's body.

PATTERSON. (*Startled*) Well—you got 'em, too.

ANNA. Was the body there, Paul?

PAUL. No—it was not. While I was looking for it—someone slugged me.

PATTERSON. What's all this about?

ANNA. I told you—but you wouldn't believe me.

PATTERSON. Yes, I believe anything *you* say.

ANNA. But I—— (MAMMY *enters.*)

PATTERSON. You're all right now—Miss West. Young man, *you'd* better not drink any more. (PAUL *sees* MAMMY *and crosses to her. Then he asks her a question.* MAMMY *nods—and points to the north.* PAUL *nods satisfaction and tells her something.* MAMMY *exits.*) I'll look in to-morrow. Everything will be all right then. Both of you have been seeing things. (*Goes to* ANNABELLE *and feels her pulse.*) Just to check up!

PAUL. (*Returns to* ANNABELLE *and* PATTERSON —*crosses to* ANNABELLE) Pulse normal, Doctor?

PATTERSON. No—take care of yourself, Miss West. I'll drop in to-morrow.

ANNA. But Paul's head——

PATTERSON. He's all right. Does it hurt you?

(PAUL *puts his hand to his head.*)

PAUL. No.

PATTERSON. (*Looks at bottle*) It never does. Good-morning. (*Exits, closing door.*)

ANNA. You say that—it wasn't there.

PAUL. No—but someone else was. Who could it have been? (*Crossing* L.) Who the dickens could it have been? (*Groans a little.*) Oh, my head begins to hurt now.

ANNA. (*Soothes him—rises and crosses* c.) There—there—don't try to think. (*Leading* PAUL *to sofa.*)

PAUL. (*Looks at her—owlishly from the blow —and the booze—he is just a trifle stunned.* ANNABELLE *brings him over to sofa and sits him down*) I've just got to think, I've just got to think. I've just got to think! Just as I had the dol-gone thing figured out—now it goes and gets itself all balled up again—we saw Crosby fall on the floor— didn't we? (PAUL *on sofa—*ANNABELLE R. *and* PAUL L.)

ANNA. Yes.

PAUL. He was dead—wasn't he?

ANNA. Yes —— (*Looks at him.*)

PAUL. Ha! Ha!

ANNA. What is it, Paul—what is it?

PAUL. How do we *know*—he was dead?

ANNA. Why—why wasn't he?

PAUL. I don't know. I suppose he was—but that doesn't prove it. I couldn't swear he was dead —neither could you.

ANNA. No ——

PAUL. I got an idea—maybe the whole thing was only a plant—that he was shamming all the time to frighten you and waiting in there to wallop *me?*

ANNA. (*Shakes her head*) Oh, no!

PAUL. (*Rises—unsteadily*) You don't think much of that one.

ANNA. No!

PAUL. Well, neither do I —— (*Crossing to table.*) Guess my ideas aren't coming as good as they might—since I got hit on the bean, but at that, I've had worse.

ANNA. Where's Mammy?

PAUL. She's out. I sent her on a personal er- rand of my own ——

ANNA. I wish she were here.

PAUL. (*Crosses to sofa*) Now don't worry about Mammy. (*Sits.*) I'll take care of you. You know I'll take care of you, don't you?

ANNA. Yes.

PAUL. All right. Now where was I? Oh, I know, Mammy. I sent her for a ——

ANNA. (*In sudden terror, thinks she hears something—cautions silence*) Sh! (*She and* PAUL *listen for a moment, then he looks at her.*)

PAUL. Think you—heard something? (ANNABELLE *and* PAUL *listen for a moment then*—) Oh, yes, I know. (*He looks at her.*)

ANNA. (*Trembling*) I thought I heard—a footstep.

PAUL. (*Listens*) Guess you're mistaken. I don't hear any—where was I—oh, yes, my garage ——

ANNA. Your garage. You didn't tell me about that.

PAUL. Didn't I! Well—I meant to—I've got the nicest garage in Wickford. Most of the cars in it are flivvers—but it's a good garage. One that any girl would be proud of. It's got a —— (*As* PAUL *looks at her, he shows all his love for her in his eyes, but on account of* ANNABELLE *being the heiress, he rambles around trying to tell her.* ANNABELLE *tries to help him. She shows audience she loves him.*)

ANNA. (*Softly*) Paul, did you miss me—when I left Wickford?

(*Door opens, showing hand.*)

PAUL. (*Fervently*) Did I miss you?—Did I miss you! (*Suddenly embarrassed.*) Sure I did—and when you went away—you didn't think—that some day I'd own a garage, did you?

ANNA. I hadn't the slightest idea. (*DOOR CLOSES.*) I'm glad you missed me, Paul, but why didn't you write to me?

PAUL. I didn't think you wanted to hear from me. Besides, I didn't have my garage then.

ANNA. Well, you have it now.

PAUL. Y-e-s! But you can't ask a girl to marry you just because you've got a garage.

ANNA. Why can't you? Does having a garage make you tongue-tied?

PAUL. S-see—here, Annabelle, are you making fun of me?

(*OPEN PANEL SLOWLY.*)

ANNA. No—indeed—I'm only trying to help you.

PAUL. You could have helped me more if you hadn't turned out to be the heiress.

ANNA. I'm awfully sorry, but I don't see why you should keep me from helping you—with your garage.

PAUL. But I don't need a mechanic. What I need is a wi—oh—oh—well—you wouldn't understand anyway. You've been living so long in Greenwich Village, with all those artists, you'd never be content to settle in the country, in a little cottage with a little garden around it and a ——

ANNA. Don't be too sure—I could live anywhere—anywhere with the man I loved.

PAUL. Could you—could you—honest?

ANNA. Of course I could—so could any woman —if she loved a man.

PAUL. (*After a gulp*) Annabelle, could you— could you?

ANNA. Yes? You want to tell me ——

PAUL. (*Rises and stands* L. *of sofa*) I want to tell you—about a new idea of mine—I've got an idea for a twelve-cylinder car—all twelve cylinders all in a row. That would give the crank shaft thirteen main bearings. Think of the power and flexibility.

ANNA. Very interesting—but what about your idea of getting someone to keep the little cottage for you?

PAUL. (*With determination, but hesitating*) Annabelle—would—would you —— (*Sits beside her.*)

(*Noise like body being dragged along floor. PAUL alert in a moment, remains quiet and they listen. After a moment, a curious shuffling noise is heard—like dragging footsteps.*)

ANNA. (*White—clings to* PAUL) There—hear that?

PAUL. (*With his eyes popping out—listens a moment*) Sounds like someone dragging something across the floor —— (*NOISE. REPEAT.*) It's all right, dear. (*They both listen. PAUL shakes and quivers and whispers.*) It's—upstairs. (*Points up. ANNABELLE gasps.*) I suppose I ought—to go up there, but I hate to leave you alone. (*Looks at her, showing he doesn't want to leave her alone. Pause.*)

ANNA. I'm not afraid.

PAUL. No! Neither am I —— (*Rises.*) Here, you'd better take this in case anything happens— wait a minute, I'll cock it for you —— (*Gives her revolver.*) Now all you got to do if you see some-thing is just point this at it—and pull the trigger —— (*Starts for door.*)

ANNA. (*Nods*) Yes—but you ——

PAUL. (*He takes the mould of a hero*) Never mind about me! If that's the guy that beaned me a while ago—may God help him. (*Opens door, turns, sees drink on table* L., *takes drink.*) I'll be

back in a minute. (*Glides out without a sound.
Closing door.*)

(ANNABELLE *sits on couch looking at closed door,
then looks front. All is deathly quiet.* ANNA-
BELLE *jumps up and goes to door, opens it and
looks off* L. *a second. The panel opens very
slowly.* ANNABELLE *crosses to window, then
back away a few steps, turns toward panel and
gives a little shriek.*)

ANNA. (*With a trembling hand, points gun at
panel. Her voice fails her, and she speaks like a
person in a dream*) I—I—don't know why you
are trying to frighten me but if you don't go away
—I'll —— (ANNABELLE *is about to fire the gun
to summon help.* HENDRICKS *rushes into the room.
catches her and speaks gently.*)

HENDRICKS. What is it, Miss—anything wrong?

ANNA. (*Clings to him frantically, sobs her relief
and points to dark corner, where monster is crouch-
ing*) There! There!

HENDRICKS. (*Shows his astonishment as he sees
him*) Gee—just in time—I knew he was around
here —— (*Takes gun.*) Close call, Miss. Don't
worry—he can't get you now—he knows me—he's
afraid of me. (*Crosses over* R. *between chair and
sofa.* HENDRICKS *goes toward monster and speaks
soothingly.*) Come on—old-timer—I've got you—
and you and me are going home—come on—come
on—I won't hurt you. Sure! He knows me all
right—and he won't try no monkey tricks.

ANNA. Oh!

HENDRICKS. Now, Miss, everything is all right
—and I'll just take him along to the asylum.
(*Panel opens wider and monster comes out slowly.
To monster.*) Come on, you—and no funny busi-

ness. (*Monster starts for door.*) Come on! Move
along faster, can't you? That's it, go **on.**

(*Monster is* R. *of door now.*)

ANNA. (*As monster is gliding toward the door
—she sees it for the first time—out of the shadow.
She darts forward, and with a quick movement,
before* HENDRICKS *can stop her—she pulls the
Benda mask off the head of the monster—revealing
the face of* CHARLIE WILDER. *She gasps*) Charlie!!

(CHARLIE, *snarling like a trapped ghost, grabs her
by left arm.* HENDRICKS *claps his hand across
her mouth, shutting off her screams, and then
the two men slam her down on the couch and
hold her there.*)

CHARLIE. (C.) How did she get wise?
HENDRICKS. (*Holding her down* L. *of sofa—he
is back of sofa*) How do I know? I got her—
just as she was going to blow the gat.
CHARLIE. Sure, she did a dance with them down
in Greenwich Village. What did you do with
Crosby?
HENDRICKS. Rolled him under the bed. (ANNA-
BELLE *tries to scream.*) Oh, shut up! Another yip
out of you and I'll ——
CHARLIE. (*Starts for door*) I'll get him if it's
the last thing I ——
HENDRICKS. No, no more killing. I did everything you told me. I planted the gong—made 'em
think I was from the asylum and locked her in the
room and while I was doing that, you got one of
your crazy spells and croaked the old man.
CHARLIE. What!
HENDRICKS. And—if we're caught—I don't go

to the chair with you—oh, no, I'll squeal—and save my own neck. (ANNABELLE *tries to scream.*) Shut up. What's the matter with you? What are we going to do with her?

CHARLIE. (*Suddenly shows a venomous, unnatural hate for* ANNABELLE) I'd like to ——

HENDRICKS. No—I won't stand for it—do you hear—I won't have it—we'll tie and gag her and put her up there —— (*Nods toward bookcase.*) I knew you couldn't drive this girl mad! From now on, it's fifty-fifty—I want half of that necklace—and then I go my way—and you go yours. I'm through with you—do you get me? (ANNABELLE *tries to scream.*) Aw, shut up, will you!

CHARLIE. (*Pays no attention to* HENDRICKS, *but is staring at* ANNABELLE *with the grin of hate on his face*) I'll make you scream, damn you! You cheated me out of my inheritance. You didn't know that I used to play around this house when I was a kid, did you? Well, I was the old man's favorite—he showed me the secret passage—and I should have been his heir, too—I *am* the next heir —see, there's my name—my name —— (*Pulls out* CROSBY's *envelope and shows it to her. Voice gradually works up to a hysterical pitch.*)

HENDRICKS. Can it! You're getting one of your spells ——

(*Here* CHARLIE *suggests that he might be the one in the family who is really unbalanced.*)

CHARLIE. When I opened that safe and read the will—I found out you had robbed me—yes, robbed me. You thought I went for the police— ha, ha! Well, I didn't, and here's your necklace! (*Shows necklace.*)

HENDRICKS. I want my half now.

CHARLIE. Try to get it.

HENDRICKS. Oh! Double-cross, eh? Well, I'll take it all. Come on, kick in! (*Pointing revolver.*)

(CHARLIE *drops necklace and* HENDRICKS *stoops down for it and* CHARLIE *grabs his gun arm and makes him drop it.* HARRY *enters.* ANNA-BELLE *sees him and shouts.*)

ANNA. Harry! (*Rushes into his arms.*)

(CHARLIE *makes rush to door and meets* HARRY, *who covers him with gun.* PAUL *comes through panel and makes a leap at* HENDRICKS, *lands on his shoulders, and pins arms.* MAMMY *enters.*)

PAUL. (*To* HARRY) Thank God you're here—I'm scared to death.
HARRY. Scared?
PAUL. Maybe.
HENDRICKS. I didn't kill him. He did it. He's been getting crazier and crazier. Just now he had one of his spells and tried to kill me.
HARRY. Tell that to the Judge. Come on, you fellows, the police are waiting—remember—I'll shoot! Now move!
PAUL. (*To* HARRY) Team work.

(CHARLIE *and* HENDRICKS, *still holding up their hands, exit, followed closely by* HARRY.)

MAMMY. It's all right, Mr. Paul. (MAMMY *exits.*)
ANNA. (*To* MAMMY) What's all right? (*Turns to* PAUL.) What's all right, Paul?
PAUL. You see, that was just another little idea of mine. I thought—that is, I got to thinking, after what you'd been through to-night that maybe you

wouldn't be so nervous if you were to wake up suddenly and found me your husband.

ANNA.   What?

PAUL.   I mean found me by your side.

ANNA.   *What?*

PAUL.   I mean in the same room ——

ANNA.   *Oh!*

PAUL.   I mean in the next room.

ANNA.   Oh! (*Relieved.*)

PAUL.   *I thought* that maybe you wouldn't be so nervous, so I sent Mammy. *I sent Mammy* for a minister.

ANNA.   Oh, Paul, you did have an idea, didn't you? (*They embrace.*)

CURTAIN

SCENE PLOTS

Acts I and III

A library in an old estate on the Hudson. It is set with panelled walls of dark brown. Bookcases extend from c. back to R. and down R. to jog and out to end of jog.

In center of bookcases (back) there is a secret panel, which is a section of the bookcases, 6 feet, 2 inches by 3 feet. This opens on hinges like a door and is controlled by a rod on top so that it can be worked from off stage. When panel is open, there is a hanging piece of black cloth on back of set to mask anyone standing there. Through this, two slits are cut for hands to reach through.

At L. C., (back) a door swinging inward. This opens out to a hallway, and across the hall is another door, swinging up. Interior backing for second (up stage) door. Rugs on both sides of up stage door.

At C. (back) an oil painting of an old gentleman. Standing below this, a small gate-leg table.

At R., above jog, a side chair. Down R. C., a sofa (high-backed Victorian) with two cushions, set obliquely. At R. of sofa, a small table. At L. of sofa, and somewhat above it, a high-backed armchair.

Down R. a safe in the wall, with a small door swinging on stage.

Down L., a window with exterior backing. Dark green portières for window. Down L. C., a library table. Side chair to R. of table and armchair to L. of table.

98

ACT II

An old bedroom in the same house, same dark color as ACTS I and III. A door up R. C., swinging on stage. Hallway backing for this door, with another door set in backing and swinging off. Interior backing for the up stage door.

At L. C., back, a secret panel. This is a sliding panel, three feet wide, which is lifted high enough for a man standing up to fall through. In this panel is a small hinged door, about 14 inches square, cut one foot above the height of the *pillows* on bed, opening up stage end off L.

Down L., a fireplace and mantel. In mantel, near down stage end, is a small receptacle with hinged door opening on stage and up, in which necklace is secreted.

Immediately to L. of secret panel, a four-poster bed. Beneath panel, a rug. Large rug for fireplace. Coal scuttle at up stage end of fireplace.

In upper R. corner, a grandfather's clock. Below clock, a dresser with side chair. Down R. C. a side chair with lady's traveling-bag. Side chair to R. and below bed. Armchair L. and below side chair. Stool down L. C., near fireplace.

PROPERTY PLOTS

Act I

OFF STAGE (L.):
Decanter of Scotch.
2 highball glasses.
Silver tray.
Sealed envelope with letter.
Bunch of keys.
Small bell (door-bell effect).
Straight jacket.

NEAR PANEL (off R.):
Benda mask (old man).
Old overcoat.
Black stockings (footless) to cover CHARLIE's
cuffs.

IN SAFE:
3 large sealed envelopes with enclosures, (will,
etc.) in brown envelope portfolio.

IN PANEL DOOR:
3 books.

ON GATE-LEG TABLE:
2 books and bronze statuette.

ON SMALL TABLE (R.):
Book and ash tray.

ON LIBRARY TABLE:
Telephone and small book.

Act II

ON DRESSER:
Smelling salts.
2 candlesticks.

BED:
    Spring mattress and cover.
    Sheet.
    2 pillows and pillow cases.
    Comforter.

ON MANTEL:
    Bronze piece.

IN MANTEL (PANEL):
    Jewel case with necklace (sapphires and
        rubies).

OFF STAGE (R.):
    Glass of water.
    Metronome (clock tick).
    Flashlight.
    Small book with letter inside.

ACT III

OFF STAGE (L.):
    Pencil flashlight.
    Doctor's medicine kit (small).
    Roll of one-inch surgeon's tape (adhesive
        plaster).
    1 roll, gauze.
    1 bottle, smelling salts.
    2 automatics.
    1 glass of water.

OFF STAGE (R.) NEAR PANEL:
    Necklace.
    Large envelope.
    Mask.
    Overcoat.
    * Board 2 feet square, covered with sandpaper.
    * Block of wood, covered with sandpaper.
        * Effect of dragging body across floor.

LIGHT EQUIPMENT

Up stage must always be in shadow.
8 250 Watt hanging baby spots.
1 250 Watt stand baby spot.
1 1,000 Watt stand spot.
1 6 foot strip with 5 blue lamps.
1 4 foot strip with 1 dark amber lamp.
2 table lamps with shades, 4 10 Watt frosted amber lamps.
1 telephone bell off stage L.
1 panel with 2 60 amp. switches and cable.
2 6 way plugging boxes.
2 30 foot cables for table lamps.

Colors for Lamps:
.Dark amber in baby spots, extreme R. and L.
Straw in other six.
Stand baby spot—amber and frost.
NO FOOTLIGHTS USED THROUGHOUT PLAY.

LIGHT PLOTS

Act I

NOTE: Upper part of stage must be kept free from direct light.

At rise: 4 baby spots R. with table lamp.
On cue: 4 spots L. with table lamp on.
On cue: 4 spots R. with lamp off.
On cue: 4 spots L. with lamp off.

Act II

3 baby spots (250 Watt) on stand in fireplace. Fire grate.
2 3 light candelabra with rose shades.
6 25 Watt ball lamps—amber for above.
1 1,000 Watt spot on stand, blue (as in other acts).
1 250 Watt baby spot on stand, amber (pin spot).
1 2 foot strip with 10 Watt dark amber lamp.
1 dummy switch L. of door.

At rise: 4 baby spots in border with candelabra on.

1st cue: 4 baby spots in border with candelabra off.

2nd cue: 4 baby spots in border with candelabra on.

Act III

Rise: Dark stage.
1st cue: 4 spots and lamp L. on.
2nd cue: 4 spots and lamp R. on.

The eight baby spots are hung on a pipe and have mats to prevent light hitting the back of set. The direct rays shouldn't reach higher up stage than half-way between sofa and set on R. and half-way between library table and set on L.

The 4 spots L. work with table lamp L.

The 4 spots R. work with table lamp R.

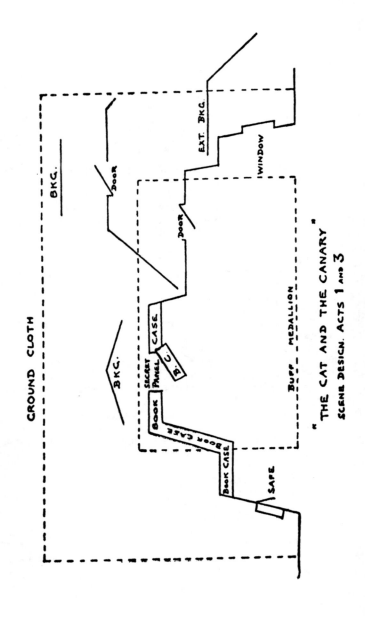

GROUND CLOTH

"THE CAT AND THE CANARY"

SCENE DESIGN. ACTS 1 AND 3

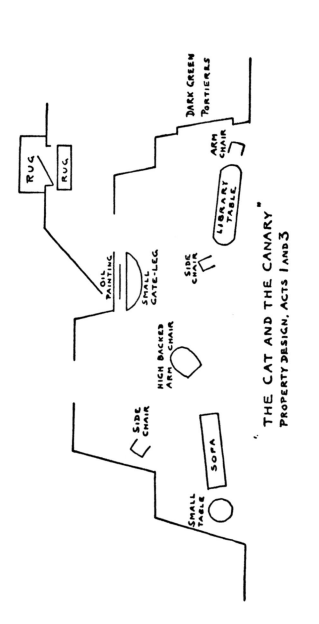

RUG

RUG

OIL PAINTING

DARK GREEN PORTIERLS

ARM CHAIR

LIBRARY TABLE

SMALL GATE-LEG

SIDE CHAIR

HIGH BACKED ARM CHAIR

SIDE CHAIR

SOFA

SMALL TABLE

" THE CAT AND THE CANARY "
PROPERTY DESIGN. ACTS I AND 3

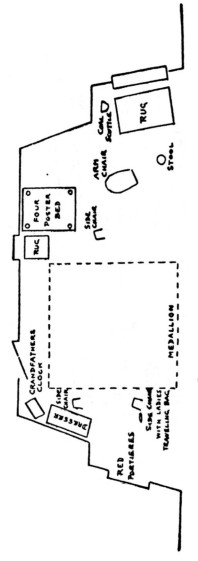

"THE CAT AND THE CANARY"
PROPERTY DESIGN, ACT 2

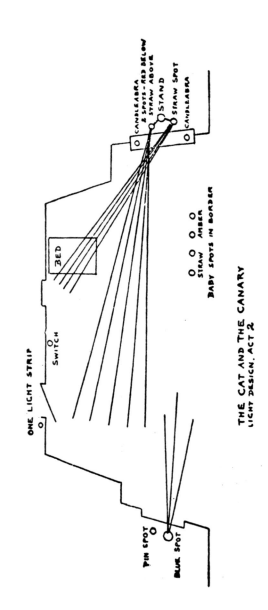

THE CAT AND THE CANARY
LIGHT DESIGN. ACT 2

ONE LIGHT STRIP

SWITCH

BED

CANDLEABRA
& SPOTS - RED BELOW
STRAW ABOVE
STAND
STRAW SPOT
CANDLEABRA

STRAW AMBER
BABY SPOTS IN BORDER

PIN SPOT
BLUE SPOT

OTHER TITLES AVAILABLE FROM SAMUEL FRENCH

VERONICA'S ROOM
Ira Levin

Thriller / 2m, 2f / Interior

This chilling mystery thriller by the author of *Rosemary's Baby* explores the thin line between fantasy and reality, madness and murder. Students Susan and Larry find themselves as guests enticed to the Brabissant mansion by its dissolute caretakers, the lonely Mackeys. Struck by Susan's strong resemblance to Veronica Brabissant, long- dead daughter of the family for whom they work, the older couple gradually induce her to impersonate Veronica briefly to solace the only living Brabissant, her addled sister who believes Veronica alive. Once dressed in Veronica's clothes, Susan finds herself locked in the role and locked in Veronica's room. Or is she Veronica, in 1935, pretending to be an imaginary Susan?

"Like being trapped in someone else's nightmare...jarring and (with a) surprising climax...a neat, elegant thriller."
– *Village Voice*

OTHER TITLES AVAILABLE FROM SAMUEL FRENCH

DANGER- GIRLS WORKING
James Reach

Mystery Comedy / 11f / Unit Set

At a New York girl's boarding house, there is a newspaper woman who wants to write a novel, a wise cracking shop girl, the serious music student, a faded actress, a girl looking for romance, the kid who wants to crash Broadway and other boarders. The landlady, is the proud custodian of the "McCarthy Collection," a group of perfect uncut diamonds. When it disappears from the safe, the newspaper woman is given two hours to solve the case before the police are called. Suspicion is cleverly shifted from one to the other of the girls and there's a very surprising solution.

CAPTIVE
Jan Buttram

Comedy / 2m, 1f / Interior

A hilarious take on a father/daughter relationship, this off beat comedy combines foreign intrigue with down home philosophy. Sally Pound flees a bad marriage in New York and arrives at her parent's home in Texas hoping to borrow money from her brother to pay a debt to gangsters incurred by her husband. Her elderly parents are supposed to be vacationing in Israel, but she is greeted with a shotgun aimed by her irascible father who has been left home because of a minor car accident and is not at all happy to see her. When a news report indicates that Sally's mother may have been taken captive in the Middle East, Sally's hard-nosed brother insists that she keep father home until they receive definite word, and only then will he loan Sally the money. Sally fails to keep father in the dark, and he plans a rescue while she finds she is increasingly unable to skirt the painful truths of her life. The ornery father and his loveable but slightly-dysfunctional daughter come to a meeting of hearts and minds and solve both their problems.

OTHER TITLES AVAILABLE FROM SAMUEL FRENCH

OUTRAGE
Itamar Moses

Drama / 8m, 2f / Unit Set

In Ancient Greece, Socrates is accused of corrupting the young with his practice of questioning commonly held beliefs. In Renaissance Italy, a simple miller named Menocchio runs afoul of the Inquisition when he develops his own theory of the cosmos. In Nazi Germany, the playwright Bertolt Brecht is persecuted for work that challenges authority. And in present day New England, a graduate student finds himself in the center of a power struggle over the future of the University. An irreverent epic that spans thousands of years, *Outrage* explores the power of martyrdom, the power of theatre, and how the revolutionary of one era become the tyrant of the next.

OTHER TITLES AVAILABLE FROM SAMUEL FRENCH

THE DECORATOR
Donald Churchill

Comedy / 1m, 2f / Interior

Marcia returns to her flat to find it has not been painted as she arranged. A part time painter who is filling in for an ill colleague is just beginning the work when the wife of the man with whom Marcia is having an affair arrives to tell all to Marcia's husband. Marcia hires the painter a part time actor to impersonate her husband at the confrontation. Hilarity is piled upon hilarity as the painter, who takes his acting very seriously, portrays the absent husband. The wronged wife decides that the best revenge is to sleep with Marcia's husband, an ecstatic experience for them both. When Marcia learns that the painter/actor has slept with her rival, she demands the opportunity to show him what really good sex is.

"Irresistible."
– London Daily Telegraph

"This play will leave you rolling in the aisles....
I all but fell from my seat laughing."
– London Star

CPSIA information can be obtained at www.ICGtesting.com
Printed in the USA
BVOW05s1039250214

345948BV00017B/497/P

9 780573 606847